Had Other Plans

Stories

Jorge Majfud

Humanus
San Diego-Acapulco

as words pass by
and these pages pass
the hours
the years
life passes
but something remains
in every word
something remains of all that has passed

Stories of a Storyteller

Stories of a Novelist

Stories of an Essayist

Stories of a Storyteller

Desire

I did not invent this story. It is a story that was once told in many forms, but it always told, more or less, the same thing. Then, due to the urgency of recent centuries, it fell into oblivion. Like the stories that matter, it may not be true, but it is truthful.

They say that two thousand five hundred years ago, there was a very good man who, on a dark night, received a visit from God. He couldn't see Him, but he could hear Him.

The man was frightened because the voice was not of this world. Immediately, he knew it was God, who had heard his prayers and had, at last, decided to speak to him.

The good man had fallen ill and was alone, abandoned, so God offered to grant him a wish.

His heart raced, but before he could say anything, God continued: "You have always been a compassionate man. In your prayers, the men and women of your village have never been absent. So, whatever you ask for yourself, I will give twice as much to each of them."

The man fell silent and, after a moment of thought, said:

"Very well. Take one of my eyes."

Jacksonville, 2018

The Full Weight of the Law

On the morning of July 27th, the newspapers and television reported a strange crime committed in Sayago. Two homeless men had killed a third, likely the night before. Though not alarming, the news surprised many. The reasonable thing, and what is most common, is to kill for money, pride, or some family passion. And none of these things could apply to a half-man who lived in the city's garbage dumps.

The exact reason for the beating was never known; and no one wanted to know more once the judge sentenced the killers to ten years in prison. But I, the judge, never entirely forgot the case, and some years later, I visited the prisoners in jail. I did it almost in secret, as with everything, because people liked to say that I favored criminals over victims. Now, if I had to pass sentence again, I would give them another ten years in prison; not for justice, but out of compassion. I believe I can explain myself.

The dead homeless man was Dr. Enríquez, who had lived without a home for the last six months. Eusebio Enríquez was a surgeon and had lost his eldest daughter in an operating room on January 24th, where he himself had intended to relieve her of an incurable illness. The surgeon had no reason to blame himself for his daughter's death, but reasons mattered little because, suddenly, he went mad and one night left his home. He crossed the city in the January rain and abandoned himself by the railroad tracks in Sayago. He let his beard grow, dirtied and faded his clothes; he quickly lost weight, and his face grew darker and more sunken, giving him the unfamiliar appearance of a *Hindu sannyasin*. He became so marginalized from society that he ceased to exist for the government and for society; and that is why they could never find him. Soon after, he met Facundo and Barbarroja, the two men who would later beat him to death with iron bars.

Neither Facundo nor Barbarroja were criminals, but people feared them or, rather, avoided them, as if poverty were contagious. While there were people who believed in God or in Hell, there were alms. But, little by little, good conscience and the tax on evil diminished, and these wretched men became part of the national unconscious, the hidden shame of a prosperous or pretentious economy.

The two men lived a nearly nomadic life. They inhabited any and all corners of the old train station, always avoiding the guard who might catch them sleeping in an abandoned train car or in the iron storage shed where they took refuge on rainy days. "This place is sad," Enríquez would say to himself, "the good thing is that they don't know it."

But, I repeat, neither of them was capable of killing a bird. It is also true that during those six months of living together, Enríquez spoke to them only once. Still, the beggars held no grudge against him. They knew he was a poor madman who had once lived like ordinary people, who must have had a house and a car and even a family, because they had seen him flee from an elegant woman in clean clothes. They had learned to live with him like a family that has a mute or disabled member. Once, when the cold was unbearable and their jaws began to tremble, they brought him a can of boiling herbs. And he did not refuse it.

But that winter was one of the worst the beggars could remember. Temperatures dropped below zero; puddles froze over by morning, and the grass turned white with frost. It became increasingly difficult, if not impossible, to find glass bottles, much less sell them. Because people avoided those men whose beards and clothes worsened with each year. And so, little by little, they lost the little oral contact that connected them to the world.

Barbarroja fell ill from hunger, and Facundo began to complain all night about rheumatism or some other indecipherable ailment. The illnesses and sufferings piled up until they blended into a single hell. Yet, the two beggars continued to wait for spring and the summer heat, which each day seemed further away. Enríquez knew it. He knew this could be the last winter for his companions: their feet were swollen and purple, their faces pale and sunken, their hands useless. Only a depressing optimism kept them going, according to him.

One morning, Enríquez opened his mouth to read them their death sentence. That day was the only time the three of them spoke, and they talked for hours. Facundo and Barbarroja learned who the madman was and almost confirmed what they had imagined. In reality, the madman was, or had been, a rich man. A petty bourgeois, to his acquaintances, but a rich man to those outcasts.

The conversation ended with a proposal from the madman.

"It will get colder," he told them, "and you will die. You no longer have defenses, and your bodies are failing. The suffering will last until September. Or, in the worst case, until October. But you will die. And if you're lucky enough to survive this year, you'll die next year, after suffering twice as much as you will this winter. But you are so poor that you don't even have ideas. You won't know how to escape this hell. Not even in the easiest way. You are so poor that you haven't even thought of going to prison, where inmates enjoy a bed with blankets and a roof and where they eat almost every day. You are so poor that you won't even have the strength to rob a market, because if you try, they'll kick you out and you'll end up with your forehead bleeding on the pavement. And if they jail you for theft, they'll release you back to the street in two days, because the prisons are full and even the judge will take pity on two miserable, starving men. But since I'm a doctor, I'm going to tell you what you must do to save yourselves."

The beggars exchanged glances, unsure of what to think. They even began to doubt the story he had told them earlier about his family and his former life.

"To go to prison for many years, you have to kill me. Don't look at me like idiots. Hide that honest stupidity you've been carrying around, stinking in your clothes."

Facundo and Barbarroja knew or imagined that the madman was worse than ever that day. But he kept insisting, with fanatical realism, on the convenience of sacrificing one of the three.

"God will punish us," said Barbarroja.

"God has already punished you. Can you imagine a Hell worse than this? Do you see what I'm saying? You are so poor that you have no ideas. You no longer reason. Do I have to come and tell you what to do? Besides, why would God punish someone who kills a murderer? The Bible says, 'An eye for an eye and a tooth for a tooth.' I killed a child, my own daughter. Do you feel sorry for me?"

The beggars stood up and retreated, frightened. The madman was beginning to truly scare them. Time passed, a week or two, and they didn't speak again. They didn't even approach him and avoided looking at him. On the 24th, it rained heavily. Facundo and Barbarroja moved to the abandoned shed at the station. As I said before, they only went there on rainy days because the guard would hassle them if he found them inside. On the other hand, I think they preferred the roofless train car because it was more discreet and the dark void of the shed's height didn't bother them. (Despite living on the street, I discovered that both suffered from a strange form of agoraphobia.)

That day, the madman didn't enter the shed. He stayed out in the rain all night, like a ghost with his hands in his pockets, sometimes looking up at the sky, which outlined him with lightning and erased him with the dark rain.

On the 25th, the madman, exhausted by hunger, cold, and a lack of will to live, fell unconscious. On the 26th, the beggars decided to bring him a can of boiled herbs, but he no longer responded. His gaze was lost, and he could barely move his eyelids. His skin was white and cold, with no reaction or sensitivity of any kind. Facundo pressed his ear to the madman's chest and confirmed that his heart was barely beating. Throughout the night of that day, the two men silently monitored the almost imperceptible beats of the madman's heart. They waited or cared for him with fear and anxiety. Barbarroja began to tremble as never before, his shoulders hunched, unable to control his lips, which seemed to recite a voiceless speech.

On the 27th, the madman's heart could no longer be heard, and by nightfall they thought he was dead. But he wasn't. Therefore, the coroner's conclusion was correct: Eusebio Enríquez did not die of cold or hunger; he was beaten to death by two beggars who confessed to the crime and were saved from a certain lynching outside the courthouse because the police dragged them to a van where they were dumped like trash.

Montevideo, 1996

The Day That Never Existed

JOSEPH HANLON (THE AUTHOR OF *Who Calls the Shots* and *Peace Without Profit*) had gone to Pemba for a BBC report on Nteuane Samora Machel. The son of the famous Mozambican revolutionary was conducting military exercises in the north; Graça, his mother, was in London receiving a new award and was not yet Nelson Mandela's wife.

The next day, *Joe* and his wife Teresa planned a tour of the islands and invited Nadia and me to join them, whether out of obligation or because they liked us at dinner with Nteuane. We left on a Friday or Saturday from Quizanga, on a fishing boat, and arrived in Ibo just before sunset.

I remember, as if it were tonight, that we settled into an old mansion owned by a friend of S.M. There were more than enough rooms, and I imagined Nadia would take the one facing the sea. Because there were masks and huge paintings by some unknown artist there; and because Nadia always avoided staying in the same room as me. But after I threw my suitcase onto one of the beds in the back room, she appeared and did the same. Without even consulting me, she said she was going to stay there, with me, because the masks that couldn't speak scared her.

"I promise I won't say a single '*a*' all night," I said, feigning confidence, "and I won't try to spy on you naked."

"You'd better not," she replied, searching my eyes. I felt those eyes in my mouth, deeply blue like her mother's.

"Did you do your daily report?" I asked after a while, referring to the long letters she wrote to Damián. She detailed all the landscapes she had seen during the day, avoiding (I know) mentioning my disinterested company. Perhaps she enjoyed writing to Damián more, seeing things through his eyes rather than her own; because love is one of those rare states where one is happy but also compelled to acknowledge it. I think I loved her in some way too.

"Not today," she said, throwing herself onto the bed. "I have no light and I'm tired. Besides, today is a day that never existed. Tomorrow will follow what was yesterday, since we don't know if it was Friday or Saturday... You don't mind, do you?"

"Of course not," I said without fully understanding. "You seem tired and a bit nervous."

After hesitating for a moment, she admitted: "Yes, it's true. It's been too long since I've heard from Damián. I know he'll be worried too."

"And with good reason," I added. "If I were him, I wouldn't have let you come alone."

"But I'm not alone!" she almost shouted, sitting up suddenly. However, as was her habit, she soon invited me to leave because she wanted to rest.

With the sun still shining, I went out with one of the guards to look for sugar for the tea and took the opportunity to get some *zuruma*. The guard pretended not to understand my Portuguese but, shortly after, promised me a few leaves for the evening.

When I returned at that hour, the English couple and Nadia were having tea in the courtyard, barely lit by a candle. Joe and Teresa were laughing at a story Nadia told. She must have told them about the time a minister of the Uruguayan dictatorship laughed at the Bolivian navy minister, because I heard her translate what the Bolivian had replied to his colleague:

"At what do you laugh? Don't you have a Ministry of Justice?"

By the door leading to the street, I found the shadow of the guard (I think his name was Babá or Dadá, which could be a Brazilian or African name); smiling, he told me that with this I would feel very good and that if I wanted, he could get more. Then he spoke to me about Pangane and other islands further south; he confused America with the poorer America, praised the clarity of my Portuguese, and couldn't tell me if it was *Friday* or *Saturday.*

When I returned to the courtyard (it was so dark they didn't even notice my movements) Joe told me about a dance that would take place on the island. He suggested that Nadia and I go, as I guessed he wanted to stay alone with his wife that night. Later, I was surprised that Nadia agreed to go; because everything in Africa bothered her: the smell of the quimoans, the mosquitoes of the macondes, the machismo of the macúas that forced women to carry water daily. I reminded her that even more odious was the machismo of our proud developed world, which forbade a woman from looking at a construction site or walking alone on a summer night. From that conversation, I discovered that she had always lived guarding herself against some kind of humiliation; and that behind her bare lips and clear gaze, she carried, from a very young age, a veil as hermetic as the visible one worn by some Muslim women. Or worse, because even then she was never safe among our *Latin lovers*. And that if there was an odious race in the world, it was precisely those representatives of the superior sex. When in India, Egypt, or Mozambique had she felt as threatened as in Montevideo or Chicago?

I admit that, despite the repeated darkness of that night, Nadia caught anyone's attention; more than usual. I think she had dressed up carefully; to impress, as at the Buckingham Palace party. The African sun hadn't done much to her skin; because it wasn't possible to draw out any color other than the embarrassed pink of her cheeks when someone praised the calmness of her eyes or the delicate line of her profile; and because she was so afraid of the foreign outdoors that she never went out without an excessive amount of sunscreen or mosquito repellent. It was enough for the heat to lower her blood pressure a little for her to imagine herself sunstroke or sick with malaria, surrounded by two thousand kilometers of impassable roads.

We expected drums and blacks jumping around a bonfire, and what we found was almost the same but with Madonna's music. As long as there was fuel for the prehistoric generator, the quimoans and Nadia danced like animals.

But the light and music didn't arrive until midnight. Just before, they faded out in an almost African roar. Until everything was left as if in a dark room. Slowly, some things began to become distinguishable, especially when the moon emerged from behind the clouds: the sea, a huge *cajueiro* tree that bordered the yard from above, the bamboo wall, some dark faces with enormous white smiles, almost always women eager to try something.

I went out into the street and took the main road, which was like a wide, sandy avenue, bordered on both sides by thick black trees and ruins of two-story buildings, almost all abandoned. I didn't find Nadia, nor did I look for her. Was I supposed to take care of her? I think I felt both anger and liberation at the same time. I rolled the "Mueda cigar" and smoked it as I walked toward the square. I entered the square and walked through all the shadows, confirming that there was no one there either, as if the entire population preferred the *palhotas* in the jungle to the old Portuguese palaces. Then I took one of the side

15

streets and walked until I reached another shadow on the sand. Suddenly, I noticed ghost-like figures. Some people were gathered around something, murmuring in Quimoa in silence. Then I approached to see that they were surrounding Nadia, lying on the white and dark sand while a man mounted her. I'm sure she saw me and saw the others watching her. And I'm almost certain she was smiling or making a gesture that wasn't one of pain. The man was one of the house guards, the same one who had accompanied us to the dance and the same one she killed. Because it was she who killed him with a skewer, not me, as she tried to make me believe the next day. But that doesn't matter at all; because that day was the day that never existed, and no one will ever know. Besides, what the guard had sold me wasn't *zuruma* but leaves from another plant whose name I no longer remember. My dear Nadia was also mistaken about this.

Pemba, 1997

The Belly of the Beast

It's night, or dusk. G. has sat down, as he does every day at 7:00 PM, in his library armchair, with a glass of whisky without ice, and watches the new television that a traveler gave him in exchange for an uncollectible debt. He watches it without enthusiasm; the novelty doesn't appeal to him. A woman smiles, emerges from the sea, and gets into a convertible. He takes a long sip and feels that warmth again, which in a few more minutes will leave him completely relaxed, fleetingly happy, as if his sadness had been just a mistake, an unjustified state of mind. A man pulls out a revolver and points it at the viewer, or at the screen, or at a camera that might now be broken and archived in some basement in London. James Bond, Agent 007, licensed to kill. G. likes that music, because it's not playing now; it's playing in some indecipherable time. Túru-túrun-túru. The woman is beautiful and doesn't worry in vain. Everything ends well. Now the music comes from the Caribbean or a Greek island. G. can't quite figure it out; but it doesn't matter. The image of those waves is beautiful, eternal. Maybe the alcohol has already taken effect. He smiles, relaxes again, and then furrows his brow in concern: someone is knocking with the brass knocker on the front door.

He immediately remembers the letter they left under his door the other night:

"From the moment you receive this sole warning, start trembling. Not praying, because we know you're a godless son of a bitch who believes in nothing."

These aren't friendly knocks, he realizes. It's been an order.

"Now we know exactly where you live and where the den is where your friends, the intellectuals who seek to ruin this country that doesn't belong to them, are hiding. We know very well where they work to spread lies about the honorable people who, whether they like it or not, will defend the Homeland from communists, Montoneros, Jews, and homosexuals. For having defied God and the Homeland, we will exterminate you like rats."

Then G. stands up, already relaxed but still sad, crosses the room with sculptures, opens the door, and sees the three of them, uniformed in authority, in arrogance.

"Mr. J. G.," he hears the first one say, the one who commands, the one who doesn't ask, the one who is above the four and enters without waiting.

G. doesn't respond. It wasn't a question, after all. The colonel enters with his fingers crossed behind his back, as those who admire Napoleon or some other military genius like to do when they're thinking about History. He pivots on his left heel and looks at him.

"Excuse me, good evening," says the colonel, almost kindly, smiling. "May we come in?"

Yes, he's relaxed, but still sad.

"What can I do for you," says G., while thinking that he must have heard that phrase last night on TV. It was a tall, dark man who had killed another and was being pursued by the police.

"We've come to pay you a visit. Routine, really. We like to go from house to house, though I confess I'd rather go to the movies," the colonel speaks loudly, as if he's used to speaking in a school for the deaf, while pacing back and forth along the same path, "but when the Homeland calls, we cannot refuse." He finishes and picks up a notepad that G. always keeps by the phone.

"Sergeant," he says, handing him the notepad, "keep it, it might be useful."

"Yes, Colonel."

Next to it, under the phone book, lies the warning letter:

"We will cleanse this country of rats, especially those rats who, like you, came down from the holds of ships. And we will continue to fulfill our patriotic duty, sending to hell those who seek to destroy the Freedom of our Nation, without waiting for faggot laws to give them time to reproduce.

"Keep your eyes wide open, don't sleep, because we will be watching you day and night to fulfill our unyielding mandate.

Freedom, Homeland, and Honor."

2.

The colonel asks for his glasses. G. hesitates, then hands them over. With a baroque gesture, the colonel tries them on, looks at his subordinates, and asks how he looks. The two approve with exaggerated smirks. Then he tries to read another book spine, avoiding touching it.

"Well, well," he says, "everything looks different this way."

This time he dares to pick up a book, opens it, and pretends to read for a photograph.

"Let's see, soldier, don't I look like an intellectual?"

"Yes, Colonel, you look like an intellectual."

"I'd say, an intelligent man."

"That's right, Colonel. You should keep Four Eyes' glasses."

"Soldier, didn't I tell you to show respect when you're in someone else's home?" the colonel scolds him. And then, pretending to try to forget it, he looks back at the book in his hands and asks:

"Tell me, Doctor..."

"I'm not a doctor, you know that."

"Well, let's say you didn't have a formal education, but to me, you're a doctor. With so many books piled up, what else could I call you? Besides, don't you teach at the University? What do you teach, Doctor?"

"Anglo-Saxon literature..." says G., almost apologetically.

"That sounds great! But tell me, professor, what is that good for?" says the colonel, looking at him triumphantly. He always comes out on top when he asks questions like that.

"What is literature good for, professor?"

G. has been thinking about the answer. An obvious question. That's why, perhaps, he never seriously considered it, and now the colonel comes to poke at the wound. Without looking at him and without breaking out of that slight introspection brought on by sadness or alcohol, G. murmurs:

"What is literature good for...? Well, for many things. But if you're concerned with utility and benefits, as I suspect from your question, I'll tell you that a narrow spirit is unlikely to harbor great intelligence. Great intelligence in a narrow spirit sooner or later ends up suffocating. Or it becomes resentful and perverse..."

G. pauses; he has probably made a mistake, albeit a trivial one: he tried to respond with an idea at a moment when any idea or reasoning is merely the scenic backdrop of an action whose outcome has already been decided in advance.

He lowers his eyebrows until they almost completely cover his eyes, while wondering what he has in common with those Vikings who crossed the North Atlantic a thousand years ago. Since childhood, he imagined them as gods who only knew the fear of others. He walked the damp paths of Fyn, where his grandfather Sune lived, surrounded by the fields of the Jørgensens, and he couldn't imagine the pain of barbarism, the frantic sweat of war, the sadness of abandonment. There, standing before him, was this uniformed man, with black hair and deliberately slow speech, who was essentially nothing more than one of those barbarians who sank ships in Nydam Mose. That man was more of a Viking than he was, who only had the blood and who dreamed every night that a group of invincible Romans had decided to kill him. G. would raise a sword with a golden hilt, as if with that gesture he were performing a magical act of his ancestors that would put his enemies to flight. But the sword became so heavy that his two arms couldn't hold it, and it fell with its tip against the floor, at which point the men with very black hair took the opportunity to approach him and surrounded him with lighter and sharper swords. And that's how they killed him. That is, that's how he would wake up with his heart pounding in his throat and ears, as if it were about to burst from the effort. More than once, G. thought he would die that way, and that people would say the next day: "he passed from one dream to the other," because people have the idea that dying in bed is one of the best ways to face the inevitable, when in reality it can be one of the most violent ways to die, an unreal way, a victim of a fiction that ends with a knock on the door or an accidental noise in the street, putting an end to the mother of all fictions, which is life.

On the television, a man speaks directly to the camera with a microphone that covers his entire mouth and part of his nose. He seems worried. He turns and asks something to someone next to him:

"How do you feel in the team?"

"Well, honestly, good. Getting here is the greatest thing that can happen to a football player, because a big team like Peñarol is the greatest there is, really."

G. reaches for his bottle of whiskey. He's not nervous. He's just sad and would definitely like to get drunk.

"How's the relationship with the other teammates? Do you feel comfortable, do you get along with all of them?"

"What, it's not good enough for us?" the colonel reproaches him, changing his tone.

"Yes, of course."

"I see you're not very polite with your guests. Why do I bother teaching my boys good manners if we're in the house of someone with no manners? As always, lots of culture and little education, as the General says."

"Honestly, yes, the camaraderie is very good, and I think we're all preparing very well to push the team forward, just as the people want."

G. pours whiskey for three more. He hands one to each, except for the one who's busy wandering around the library. He has a square jaw that stands out from the rest of his face. He looks carefully and pulls a book from a shelf that's against the floor and asks, Colonel, what language is this with an *o* crossed by a little stick? The colonel reads: Søren Kierkegaard, *Frygt og Baeven.* He reads with difficulty. He doesn't understand and gets annoyed. He throws the book on the desk and declares: it's Russian, soldier, some Bolshevik crap.

"It's Danish," says G.

"It's Russian," orders the Colonel. "If I tell you it's Russian, it's Russian, you hear me, shit?"

"It's Russian," repeats G. He's thinking about the second drawer of his desk. For a moment, he looks at it. When he's completely drunk, he'll be able to do it. It shouldn't be that hard: just put the barrel to his temple and pull the trigger. Maybe it'll hurt less than the dentist. No one will mourn him, except for Gutiérrez, who's still waiting for a check he couldn't cover last Friday. He just has to wait for the right moment, because they won't let him kill himself so easily. First, he has to suffer, my Colonel, he has to eat his mother's shit, what's the big deal, after all, you know very well why we're here, don't you?"

"No, not exactly."

There's a rumor that the coach is very demanding with the team and that Pato Lima might be sidelined because of the missed penalty in the last match—a slow-motion image shows a Peñarol player with his hands on his waist, adjusting his body as he waits for the referee's order. He's chewing gum, which doesn't match the calm image he's trying to project—. *What does a center-half like you, who's been coached by so many managers before, think?*

Well, I think Pato is a great player and an excellent person, and some of the things said on the field are just the heat of the moment. But with a cooler head, I think everything will work out, and Pato will return to the team —He takes a run-up, floating in the air of that night, approaches the ball, and kicks it. The ball takes a moment to leave his foot, and when it does, it transforms into a misshapen white rugby ball, until the goalkeeper stops it, almost effortlessly.

As we watch the images of that fateful moment for Pato, we'd like to know, from the studio, what Almeida thinks about the coach's position regarding everything that's been said about the Pato Lima-Pastoriza case.

Understood, understood. I'll pass the question: Pastoriza López?

We don't get along very well with the coach. Just the other day, we were talking with Cabeza, and we were saying how incredible it is how clear the coach is in his talks and how well he gets his point across about what he wants.

The Colonel approaches G., slowly, with his hands hanging behind him.

What's the coach's plan for this difficult test that's coming up?

He looks at him for a moment, somewhere between ironic and about to explode.

Well, he always tells us to play football, to push forward, and when we lose the ball, to try to recover it.

"What are you playing at?"

"I don't know," says G., almost drunk, completely sad, "but I'm getting used to it. Three men arrive, break through the ceiling of my room looking for weapons or money, insult me. Sometimes they spit in my face and then leave. In the end, they always come back."

"Oh, the little gentleman is upset because the institution, Safeguard of the Homeland, spits in his face. And you, don't you spit on our flag?"

G. doesn't respond. He pours himself more whiskey and tries to move closer to the second drawer of the desk. But the Colonel orders him to sit in the chair that's just been vacated. The flag. G. leans back and feels the warmth left by the soldier. It's body heat, like any other. G. only thinks about the second drawer. He doesn't care what the Colonel might be saying about rights and duties to the homeland.

"In every State Institution," reflects the Colonel, "they should put a sign at the entrance with the First Law: *When the Homeland is in danger, there are no rights for anyone. Only obligations.* That's what Socrates should have said, the one who died for his homeland."

"But wasn't Socrates a philosopher?" asks one of the soldiers.

"Of course, but he died for his homeland. There are also philosophers who defend the homeland. Socrates was a subversive, and he killed himself by drinking poison. That's what all traitors should do."

Thanks, Jaime. Good luck to the boys from Peñarol, and welcome to Argentina. Good luck to our Independiente too, Pepe.

Of course, we hope the Red Devils are blessed with better fortune in the next match and that they represent us well as a Nation.

I'm sure they will, Pepe, given the history of the red institution..."

Of course. We must also not forget that, by some mystery of Fate, it has fallen to Independiente to be the club that has won the Copa Libertadores of America the most times.

Something to reflect on, truly. We send you our regards. Goodbye.

"G. tries to stand up, but the Colonel places a hand on his shoulder and pushes him back into the armchair.

From sports, we now move to the international scene...

"Let's get to the point," he says. "I'll tell you, since you claim not to know, why we're here. We found out that you traveled to Montevideo on the 14th. You can't trust a cleaning lady; you should fire her... Isn't that right?

"I should fire her," says G., while watching as somewhere in the world a ten-story building collapses and a river overflows, carrying a dead cow in its current.

"You traveled to Montevideo, yes or no.

"Yes," says G., and then confirms, unnecessarily: "I went to Montevideo."

Behind the cow floats a man who is still alive, because he tries to grab onto an electrical cable. His hand slips from the cable, and the body disappears.

"Yes, yes. We know you went to Montevideo. Old news. But what we want to know is something else," says the Colonel, pacing back and forth with his fingers crossed over his buttocks. "Didn't you know that you can't travel to Montevideo without special permission?

"Yes.

"But you didn't have any special permission, and yet you took a little trip to the "tacita del Plata."

"Yes. I requested that special permission from your superiors, and they denied it.

"In Mar del Plata I'm happy," goes the song... *We're in direct contact with Mar del Plata. Stay alert, Luisito, stay alert. Can you hear me?*

"Well, the *how* we already know: you falsified documents. What remains is the most important part: the *why*. What did you go to Montevideo for?

"I went to find a woman.

"Damn, the Jew turned out to be a romantic," says the Colonel, feigning surprise. G. doesn't correct the racial confusion. "Please, Mr. G., I just had a snack, a cappuccino with croissants at the corner café, while we waited for you to arrive. Do me a favor, don't ruin my digestion. In three years, I'll retire, but don't think I'll wait three years to pass on to a better life. I'll be honest with you: I have a principle of not stressing myself out. I think things should be handled as calmly as possible, with composure, there's no need to shout to give an order. In that, I'm like you; I don't like raising my voice. Whether I do my job well or poorly, I still get the same salary. So, I don't plan to complicate myself too much at work, nor will I do overtime with a shitty Jew who thinks he's clever. I suggest you don't keep us here until nine at night, which is when my shift ends, because I might start getting in a bad mood.

G. isn't listening, he's lost the thread of the military's reasoning. He manages to stand up and approaches the whiskey bottle, which he now places on top of the second drawer. He knows that if he doesn't grab it in time, they'll find it. And it will be soon, because the soldier with the pelican jaw is still rummaging behind the books. He'll move to the desk and open the second drawer. G. remembers a man he met in Zárate, with a jaw like that. He'd been operated on, and they'd filed the bone several times, but the jaw kept growing. He was a waiter in a bar.

"That's right," he says, as if to himself. "I went to find a woman, in Montevideo.

"Listen here, you son of a bitch," the Colonel interrupts him, pressing his index finger into G.'s cheek, "cut the nonsense. No one takes risks like that for a woman. We're in the 20th century, you understand?"

"Yes, I understand, *perfectly,*" says G., emphasizing the last word to himself. In the 20th century, you don't kill or die for such things. In the 20th century, people are judged for their political ideas; not for their feelings. The criminals of my party are protected, while any honest man from the opposing party can be subjected to torture, arson, or imprisonment. How can such abstractions unleash so much passion?

"Then sing. What did you go to Montevideo for?

"I went to find a woman.

3.

The bars open with a clang, and G. is led into a dark room, smelling of dampness, ashtrays, and with a lamp over a stainless-steel table. The Colonel is waiting for him, smiling, freshly shaved, with a neat, fine, and well-trimmed mustache. G. no longer thinks he looks so thin.

"Sit down, I have good news. We're going to release you, since we were able to confirm that you weren't lying. Indeed, the woman you were looking for exists. Her name is Mabel Moreno..." says the Colonel, putting on his glasses to read a report. "*Mabel Moreno Zubizarreta.* Here it says you met on a ship. The young lady was traveling with her father, from Spain. Upon arriving in Montevideo, her father died of a heart attack, probably from the distress caused by his own daughter falling in love with an anarchist vagabond, several years older than her. And you abandoned her to her fate, continuing your journey to Buenos Aires...

G. raises his eyes for the first time and directs them toward the Colonel, who is reading a paper. He can barely see him clearly because of the lamp in the way.

"Happy? You can't complain, we did the work for you. We should charge you.

"Mabel," says G., in a very weak voice, and he realizes he can barely speak. But he insists: "Mabel... Where does she live?"

"In Montevideo, right? Let's see, let me check..." the Colonel reads again with effort, leaning closer to the lamp's light. "Calle Rincón y Piedras. Neighborhood: Ciudad Vieja.

G. wants to know more, but he stays silent. He knows they'll tell him anyway.

"Aren't you asking for more details? I thought you were very interested in this woman. Otherwise, you wouldn't have risked your life crossing the river. And you wouldn't have messed with us, forcing us to personally verify that you were telling the truth. Which pissed me off a little, because I know you're involved with the big Bolshies, and I also know that one day I'm going to catch you.

The Colonel walks around, trying to think, and continues:

"As I was saying, we did the work for you, because military intelligence is superior to cultured intelligence. Congratulations, Mr. G., your woman is beautiful, a very beautiful *prostitute*.

The other four men in the room had been waiting for this moment. They fixed their gazes on G.'s downcast face. Some will say he didn't even flinch. Others will say it was clear his world was falling apart. They'll never agree.

"A beautiful prostitute who works near the port," the Colonel insists, in case the previous statement didn't sink in deep enough. "Did you know that your beloved, the woman for whom you risked your life, sleeps with other men for money?

The Colonel looks at him more closely. G. barely reacts, and the Colonel becomes furious. He shouts at him:

"You don't care!

"No..." G. responds weakly.

"Ah, you don't care," says the Colonel, straightening up, disappointed. "Maybe you'd like to know how much she charged me for half an hour. Can't guess? Three hundred Uruguayan pesos, which in our currency... I don't know how much that is. But it doesn't matter, because the State paid for it, let's say the taxpayers like you.

Definitely, there are no longer any living expressions on G.'s face. The others give up on observing him. One leaves, saying it's not worth it. The others stay because they know there's more.

"Three hundred pesos..." the Colonel reflects. "Three hundred pesos for half an hour where she was screaming like crazy, because they called me Cabo Largo for a reason, even though I was never a corporal. Maybe it doesn't bother you that your beloved is a prostitute because you don't believe us. Of course, but that's why we belong to the Argentine Army: we anticipate everything," says the Colonel, picking up a manila envelope from the table.

Inside are some enlarged black-and-white photographs. He takes them out and studies them for a moment.

"We've taken some snapshots, because the government pays us, but we have to account for our activities and expenses. What do you think? I'll show you a half-body photo, and you tell me if it's her or not.

He chooses and finally places one in front of G. It's Mabel, almost in profile, looking at the camera, a little frightened.

"Is it her, your Juliet, yes or no?

G. doesn't respond.

"Well, maybe that photo doesn't represent her well," says the Colonel. "It happens sometimes. Some photos don't look like the model. Let's see, if I show you others, maybe you'll finally recognize her."

G. doesn't respond; he only moves his eyes occasionally to confirm that it's Mabel in all the photos.

"Well, in the end, maybe it's not your Mabel. So, I can show you all of them without you being too scandalized. This one is my favorite," says the Colonel, as if admiring it for a moment before placing it fifty centimeters from G.'s face. "The one at the top, with his back turned, is Agent Fabiolo. No one would say it's Agent Fabiolo, because no one knows him by his buttocks, and the very shy guy hid his head. What a lad. Well, actually, all men are shy. Haven't you noticed that in pornographic magazines, the woman is always the one who shows her face, while the man who's with her hides his? Women always lose their shame faster. And they say shame is like virginity: once you lose it, there's no going back. Well, maybe you've never seen a pornographic magazine. Take advantage now and enjoy these film stills with us.

G. doesn't want to be seen with moist eyes; he tilts his head, trying to look away, but behind him he meets the smiling face of a soldier. The Colonel has won again, thinks the soldier.

"Don't think we forced this poor woman to do what it looks like she's doing here," the Colonel continues. "No, no, sir. That's not manly. Besides, we wouldn't want to have problems with our Uruguayan brothers. In fact, we paid her for the service, which is a job like any other. And no job is shameful. Work honors people. And look, we even gave her a few extra pesos for the photographs, which was the only thing she didn't like.

Montevideo, 2000

The Confession of a Killer

When he arrived at the Carrasco airport, the new building pleasantly surprised him. The country had forgotten the crisis and was trying to reflect its recent economic prosperity in a small but ultramodern airport, with nothing to envy from the giants of the United States and Japan.

As soon as he took a taxi and began to plunge into the chaos of Montevideo, he thought that perhaps the country hadn't changed much in recent years. The lines of the streets still seemed somewhat blurred or faded; drivers honked unnecessarily and muttered insults to themselves or shouted some obscenity out the window before speeding away.

As the week went on, he realized that things had changed a lot and very little. The differences between rich and poor remained Latin American, though, measured in monetary terms, the rich were now much richer and the poor somewhat less poor. After a hundred years of conservative governments, a long democracy, and a few dictatorships, Uruguayans were living the debated utopia of a government formed by former guerrillas.

The victory of a Tupamaro president in the last elections had left him indifferent. Since childhood, he had learned to despise the danger of overly elaborate ideas about society, and on his own, he had discovered that utopias don't die; they commit suicide. And an electoral victory was the worst thing that could happen to those crazies from the sixties who had stopped imagining a perfect world to try to avoid catastrophe.

Curiously, what had most embittered Santiago during his entire stay in the United States was the news about the 2009 referendum in Uruguay, when the people ratified, with a majority of abstentions, the old law that protected and kept the killers of the past military dictatorship unpunished. He secretly grew bitter because he never had the courage to admit, to his friends and family, that he harbored a secret and inexplicable rage for those years of which he had almost no memory. So, he didn't add anything more when Paulina wrote to him from Montevideo commenting on the news and congratulating the Uruguayan people for the wisdom of maintaining the peace and democracy that had been so hard to recover, despite the romantic stupidity of electing as president an old guerrilla who lived in a cave planting flowers.

He was lucky to enter the American Hospital, though it surprised no one. The most important medical institutions (the British, the Italian, and the Spanish) had competed for him, but the American was the one that offered the best pay and certain conditions to carry out the projects he had in mind long before receiving his PhD from Emory University.

Paulina was hopeful about the reunion. That kind of academic exile had matured the young doctor.

His parents were proud. They had rescued Santiago from a dysfunctional family in Artigas, marked by a rural culture of domestic violence and likely by his father's abuse, which had left Santiago with aggressive and entirely inappropriate behavior. Since the age of four, he had exhibited behavior that went beyond the classic tantrums typical of children his age. When he started kindergarten, he still had fits of rage, and during his school years, there was a period when he would touch his female classmates' bottoms, which caused a scandal among his teachers and led to his expulsion for misconduct. His adoptive parents transferred him to a Catholic boarding school, and the psychologist confirmed the suspicions about the bad habits of his biological parents, which was why they had lost custody. By the age of ten, he was a normal and hardworking child. He had miraculously overcome his asthma attacks and from then on stood out as the best student in his class, never getting involved in politics, not even in the eighties when the country regained democracy, nor in the nineties when he entered university.

In summary, Santiago felt in his prime upon his return. He arrived full of projects and other concerns he couldn't quite rationalize. On Saturdays, he explored the Costa de Oro area, and on Sundays, he took shorter walks through the neighborhoods of Montevideo. Less known or completely unknown, except for police reports, the peripheral areas and the older parts of the city center remained part of the collective unconscious, repressed, Santiago thought, while the luxurious and pristine apartments along the coast presented the world and their own residents with the best face of the city.

One Monday, a 69-year-old patient was referred to his office. The man (who, after hearing his full name, said his friends called him Bebe and his neighbors called him Colonel Ruiz Díaz or simply the Colonel) showed no serious symptoms in his physical appearance. On the contrary, a bright, recently restored smile and a physique accustomed to moderate exercise showed an older man, somewhat stooped but entirely healthy. Except for the coronary obstruction.

While Santiago refined his diagnosis, Bebe praised the cleanliness and space of his office. In his day, the Military Hospital was rather dark, the offices didn't smell of fruity candles, and the doctors didn't dress so elegantly.

Santiago barely looked up from the test results as he spoke. Don Bebe detailed all his preferences for morning exercise; for healthy food and black-label whiskey; for a very active sex life without any need for Viagra, though at his age he had already stopped eating out as frequently; for walks along the Pocitos promenade almost every afternoon, from five to six-thirty. He went on at length about his sadness over the decline of society since the Marxists had taken power, this time legally, which he didn't question, because elections are elections and must be respected, but undoubtedly relying on the same old lies…

When Santiago told him that surgery was inevitable, Don Bebe was surprised. He opened his eyes and immediately furrowed his brows in a questioning gesture.

"What do you mean I have to have surgery, doctor?

"There's no other way. Your aorta is blocked and needs to be replaced with one from a pig.

"A pig's?"

"Yes. Why are you surprised? Surely you know someone who's had heart surgery."

"Yes, yes. I know several. It's like an epidemic. Now everyone's having heart surgery. It wasn't like that before."

"Not everyone. And before, people just died from heart attacks. That's what we're going to avoid with timely intervention. It will improve your quality of life. You think you're healthy, but you have this problem and you're not exercising. You need surgery."

"So that's why I get so tired when I walk… right, doctor?"

"No doubt about it. You're someone who's always exercised and lived healthily. There's no reason for you to get tired walking along the promenade."

Don Bebe said he would think about it, that he needed to discuss it with Carmencita, his wife, and his three children. The risk was very low; almost no one died from heart surgery these days. But there were always cases to fill that five percent of fatalities. Besides, the mere idea of having his chest opened from top to bottom to remove his heart like in an Aztec ritual terrified him.

Unanimously, Don Bebe's family was in favor of the surgery, so the patient ran out of excuses, though he delayed the date of the operation as long as he could.

One cold morning, he felt unwell and was taken to the emergency hospital. He arrived with a pre-heart attack. Santiago treated him until he recovered. Once again, events had proven the young doctor right. By then, his reputation had spread throughout the sanatorium and beyond, among his colleagues and new patients. Carmencita, Don Bebe's wife, had repeatedly invited him to tea at their home in Carrasco so he could meet their daughter, who was just two subjects away from graduating as a pediatrician. But Santiago had repeatedly used his profession as an excuse, claiming he had no set hours or rest.

Carmencita had waged a psychological campaign to convince her husband to undergo surgery and had promised him a vacation in Miami.

"Have you been to Miami?" she asked Santiago.

"Yes, many times."

"We've never been to the United States," Carmencita complained. "Can you believe it? A career military man like my husband, who always fought for democratic values during the time of the rebels, never wanted to go to the United States. He says he doesn't know a word of English, but I think it's just an excuse."

"You don't need to know English to visit the United States," Santiago said. "Besides, in Miami, most people speak Spanish."

"Of course. Imagine, there are all the exiles from Castro's regime. My husband would have plenty to talk about with any of them. Did you hear that, Bebe? What the doctor said? In Miami, almost everyone speaks Spanish."

Bebe made a face. Carmencita continued with her usual routine:

"We're not going to die without seeing Miami. We've already been to Europe. Miami is the one thing left on my list. Or New York, why not? After you have the surgery, we'll go. And no more arguing, as you like to say. No more excuses about the language. Did you hear me, old man?"

"I'll have the surgery, but I'm not going to the United States. Just the thought of going through all those investigations to get a damn visa makes my blood boil. The Yankees think they're the cream of the crop, but they're nothing but traitors. They use you and then throw you away like a dog. They have no consistency, because while some defend freedom, other Marxists hide behind that farce of a 'country of laws' to throw even Rambo in jail. But they forget all the laws when Rambo is doing what he has to do. No, no, sir. I'd rather spend my last days among my people, here, in our little country, which I've earned after serving the homeland my whole life."

"Hallelujah! At least you're going to have the surgery, old man. That's already a lot for a stubborn grump like you…"

The surgery was scheduled for Friday, May 20th, but the Colonel canceled it at the last minute. He said he had "a very important match" that day, which left everyone puzzled. But no one dared to ask him directly and instead preferred to speculate about the Colonel's professional activities, which were still very important and confidential despite his retirement. The Colonel also enjoyed maintaining an air of mystery around himself. A nephew joked that, for once in his life, the Colonel was showing signs of weakness. Someone told him this, but he just laughed it off, as was his habit when he knew the answer but preferred not to respond.

So the surgery finally took place on Friday, June 3rd. The waiting room was filled with family and friends in uniform, and the patient showed everyone, amid jokes and laughter, that he wasn't afraid of the surgery or death.

As soon as the anesthesist had adjusted the dose that was beginning to drip, Dr. Santiago Zabala asked the anesthesist and the assistants to leave him alone with the patient to confirm his psychological state before the procedure. The assistants didn't understand what he meant but obeyed the request, more out of respect for the cardiologist's reputation than the regularity of the process.

Don Bebe tilted his head and asked if everything was alright. Santiago confirmed:

"Everything is just fine. In a few hours, you'll be even better."

"I'm in your hands, doctor. I trust in your science."

"Don't doubt it. How are you feeling?"

"Very good, a bit more relaxed. It's like I just had a little whiskey. You feel really good, little by little."

"Yes, it's something like that. Back in the day, when there was no anesthesia, they'd amputate legs with plenty of whiskey. Anesthesia not only relaxes but also helps the memory release the oldest memories. Don't you remember anything from your childhood?"

"Yes, yes… I clearly remember a horse my father gave me for my birthday, in Rivera. It was actually a pony, but to me, it was huge… I even remember the smell of the horse and honeysuckle."

"Did you ever fall off the horse?"

"I fell and landed face-first in a honeysuckle bush."

"Is that where you got that scar on your trapezius muscle?"

"Trapezius muscle?"

"The scar shaped like a Z."

"Oh, yes, this one, here by the neck…"

"Yes, that one."

"No, that one, I got it trying to climb over a barbed wire fence during training. A damn rusty barb… it hooked into my skin and, like a fishing hook, it wouldn't let go. And I, in pain, pulled on the wire to free myself and tore my skin and flesh in a terrible gash that was hard to heal later. Because of the infection, you know? The worst part was that I passed out from the pain… It was my first year in the army, and the veterans made fun of me for a year. I had to wait for the new batch of recruits to arrive to earn some respect… I had a hard time back then, but now I remember all that and it seems fantastic to me. Can you believe it?"

"It's the anesthesia. It makes you feel good even about the worst memories."

"That's right, doctor…"

"I also remember that scar. With another one like it crossed over, you'd have a perfect swastika tattoo."

Don Bebe tilted his head and looked at the doctor with drunken eyes that still revealed astonishment.

"I never forgot that scar," Santiago continued. "My parents had a farm in Artigas or Rivera. When two *jeeps* from the army arrived, my mother ran to the kitchen. I have fragmented memories. Fractured. Kid stuff. Then I remember the soldiers grabbed my father by the arms and tied a very thick rope around his chest. My mother tried to intervene, but one of them dragged her back into the house. I remember my father being dragged across the dry field, behind a horse, as if he were a plow. For a long time, I thought my father must have been more concerned with holding onto the rope tightly than with the stones and thorns tearing his body. If he let go of the rope, he'd die from suffocation. Did you know Jesus died from suffocation? That was the death of the crucified in the times of the ancient Roman Empire. The muscles in the arms would give out, and as they relaxed, the body would hang and prevent the condemned from breathing. Ironies of history: a while ago, I did a brief *research* and concluded that Che Guevara, the rebel killed by the empire of the time, also died from suffocation, undoubtedly drowning in his own blood… The screams of my mother still echo from somewhere in my memory. I was in the shed, in a very high fruit crate where the hens laid eggs. From there, I could see how they took my father first and then my mother. They put her in a *jeep*, almost naked. Finally, the two remaining soldiers searched everything, the house and the shed, until they found me hiding there. I don't remember ever crying. I only remember one of them grabbed me by the arm and took me in the *jeep* that was left. He held me tightly by the hair on the back of my neck, while I tried to tear open that Z-shaped scar. And the scar wouldn't open. My nails slipped on the sweaty skin."

Don Bebe listened with his eyes wide open, filled with terror.

"Now, Colonel, tell me where they are…"

"I don't know what you're talking about…"

"Colonel, you don't have much time. The anesthesia is taking effect. You remember that moment perfectly. You handed me over to the Zabala Méndez family. Look, I love my adoptive parents, but I want to know where my real parents are. I want to know my name, my first name.

Maybe I was called Karl or Camilo? What was my name before I was called Santiago Zabala?"

"I don't know what you're talking about."

"Look at me closely. You have only a few minutes left to make the most important decision of your life."

"Are you threatening me...?"

"Yes."

The Colonel looked the doctor in the eyes, with fearful eyes despite the drunkenness of the anesthesia.

"Alright..." he finally said, "alright. Don't get upset. I'll tell you everything. Anyway, the law protects me... I handed over the child... I mean, I handed you over to the Zavalas. The Zavalas lived in Buenos Aires and were on a waiting list, but they were very close friends with General Máximo Monzalvo... Among their preferences, they had marked 'blonde,' because they were more intelligent and the adoption would raise fewer suspicions, and... in the area, everyone knew that family had a communist son, the result of the bad influence of a student they met in medical school... an anarchist and used to the good life in the capital... We needed more clues about three escaped Tupamaros who... were trying to cross the border... I took the couple to the Rivera barracks and interrogated them myself." Two kids in their early twenties... I used the usual methods, but there was a soldier who didn't know how to measure the force of his blows... When the child was left without parents, I felt sorry for him and offered to take him to Buenos Aires myself. That trip in 1975 was hell. But we made it, and I had to hide from the Zavalas that the child suffered from asthma... The Zavalas, an excellent family... I was just following orders...

"Were you also following orders when you squeezed my father's testicles and had him dragged across the field before throwing him like a dying animal onto the *jeep*, huh? My father was tied up, and you had other armed men on your side. Is that what they taught you in the army about how to be a real man? Were you also following orders when you groped my mother and said to save her for the colonel...? But back then, you must have been just a lowly lieutenant, and you fondled her a bit before handing her over to your superior, right? Because you were already lustful, but your sense of pimping was even stronger. Forgive me if I'm unfair; back then, I was only about three years old, more or less. So this last part I deduce from a single image, the image of a woman, more precisely my mother, being dragged toward the *jeep* with her breasts exposed, surrounded by a party of men like you. And since the law still protects you and will protect you until you die (or do you think I didn't notice how worried you were about the vote in parliament on May 20?), because there's always a discount for wholesale criminals, I have no choice but to keep speculating about fragmented facts that I hold like shards of glass in my chest. Now tell me, Colonel, what did you do afterward? Was all that humiliation not enough that you also had to torture them and make them disappear, so there'd be no trace, right? Tell me, tell me, you son of a bitch... Don't fall asleep now. You still have a few minutes left...

Santiago slapped his face several times, but the patient seemed unresponsive. It was the first time he acted without calculation and committed the biggest mistake of his life. He shouldn't have wasted so many crucial seconds venting his rage. The colonel was about to reveal where they had buried his parents, but he didn't have time. He couldn't be faking it. The anesthesia took him into a deep sleep. Perhaps to that moment when the lieutenant, in his early thirties and in his best physical shape, had subdued María Ocampo in the kitchen—Santiago would never know that her last name was Ocampo and that his mother's name was María—partly by force and partly by promising mercy for her husband. Later, he learned that María had allowed herself to be raped because she knew her son was hiding somewhere in the shed. The husband had given out sooner than they expected. Not in the field but in the barracks. Don Bebe, who was a lieutenant at the time, had heard the curses of General Máximo Monzalvo, who said these damn soldiers hadn't learned anything at the School of the Americas, that for severe interrogations there were doctors who controlled how far you could go with a detainee before they broke. So both the woman and her husband broke in the hands of amateurs, without revealing anything, not even one of those fake names detainees invent to escape the electric prod. The woman (a waste, said the general, with those blue eyes and those breasts in their prime, screaming for her child instead of giving in and cooperating) died of a heart attack. At least that's what they told Bebe before assigning him a minor mission. Carmencita didn't know, but two of her retired friends guarded the secret like two graves.

At a quarter to six, Dr. Santiago Zabala appeared in the waiting room and announced that the operation had been a success. The first to hug him was Carmencita. Then his three children and his comrades-in-arms, the younger ones in uniform.

Exhausted after several hours of intense concentration, Santiago (or rather, that other man who now didn't know his name) went for a walk along the coastal promenade. He knew he would never run into the colonel walking there, but at least now he knew that what had been an obsessive nightmare all his life was his memory as a child refusing to forget. He had almost no new information; only confirmations. The truth had made its way through the collective madness and would surely die mute with him and with the colonel. A strange complicity with his parents' murderer had been established since then, amidst the labyrinth of people ("of voters, of judges," he thought) who came and went unnoticed along the promenade.

Don Bebe had a normal recovery. However, his wife said, he was never the same again. He had lost his taste for exercise and hardly ever went for walks along the promenade, except at odd hours. Dr. Santiago told him it was normal for many heart surgery patients, a certain depression easily controlled with the medication he had prescribed. The colonel's daughter, who was about to graduate as a pediatrician, confirmed it. The important thing, the doctor said, was that his life expectancy had now been extended by at least twenty or twenty-five years.

That was exactly what he told Don Bebe as soon as he opened his eyes and Don Bebe asked him why he was still alive. He told him not to imagine that the surgery had been a success because the doctor was a good man. On the contrary, he was certain that the colonel would never tell him where his parents' bones were and that there would be no justice, no national referendum, or twisted parliamentary vote that would force him to confess.

"Justice delayed is justice denied," said the doctor.

And he said he had decided to do his best work so that he would live, so that he would live a long time. Because, unlike Don Bebe and his wife Carmencita, the doctor didn't believe in hell and no longer believed in justice either.

So that was the worst thing that could happen to the colonel—that he would live, that he would live a long time, remembering what he would never confess, cursing that son of a bitch for every new day of life God gave him.

Gainesville, 2012

Sweet Revenge

From the bar on Misiones Street, they saw her hurry by, her heels clicking as usual. Willian followed her with his gaze, and Carlitos said:

"That girl gets hotter every day."

"Do you know her?" asked Willian, feigning surprise.

Deep down, Willian knew that Carlitos knew everyone, because people in small towns develop that ability to dig into and remember the life and deeds of every individual who passes by twice within fifty meters. It wasn't a matter of the number of people living in a small town or a big city like Montevideo, he thought, but of skills and interests. In small towns, like Rivera, others are always a matter of interest.

"I knew the old man, Dr. Aguirre. He had his office just a few blocks from here, right across from Plaza Matriz. Next door was the notary Juan Rossi's office."

"Did the Italian guy die?"

"About three years ago. Maybe they haven't even cremated him yet. When I met this girl, she must have been eight or nine years old."

"Does she remember you?"

"Not a chance. I've crossed paths with her a few times on Sarandí pedestrian street, and it seemed like she was even disgusted that an old man was looking at her."

"She's really pretty, that girl."

"Yeah. But I looked at her in case, by some chance, she remembered me. One day I almost greeted her, but I didn't dare. She might have snubbed me. She's always been very stuck-up. Her boyfriends were all from Carrasco, and if they weren't driving a BMW, they were in a Mercedes Benz. Now she's with a doctor from the American Hospital."

"And how do you know so much?"

"Things you just find out."

"You don't deny you're from the countryside. The years go by, you get old, and you don't lose the habits you picked up as a kid."

"On the contrary. There are things I don't forget. I always liked her mother, Dr. Aguirre's wife. Don't make that nosy face. I never crossed the line. If anything, it was Grace Kelly who crossed it a couple of times. Because women like to mess with your head and then leave you drooling like an idiot. She and Grace Kelly were like two peas in a pod. She must have known it, because she acted like it."

"And you get old and don't learn."

"Worse. You get old and get even dumber. But God bless those goddesses. After all, we're the fools, and if goddesses like that didn't exist... what would life be?"

"We'd have to pay a tax to keep them from disappearing."

"Grace Kelly, who was actually named María José, drove me crazy to the point that I often went to the notary's office just to see if I was lucky enough to run into her in the elevator. All for nothing. Like life, you know?"

"And? Come on, don't get all nostalgic and silent on me…"

"This girl, Paulina, who back then was just 'Pau,' must have learned all those tricks from her mother that the weaker sex invents to enslave brutes like us. Worse than her mother, they said."

"Who said that?"

"Dr. Aguirre's employees, who were all buddies with Notary Rossi's employees. Do you need something signed too, damn it?"

"Alright, alright. Don't get worked up…"

"She's so much like her mother that she even gave one of those fools some hope…"

"Which *fools*"?

"One of Notary Rossi's employees… I used to know his name, but I can't remember it now. A skinny kid, freckled, with broad shoulders, like one of those Mexican or Filipino boxers but freckled, featherweight type."

"And?"

"The girl had rejected him in a really bad way. Really bad. Humiliating, they said, but I can't confirm that last part. It seems he… Germán. I just remembered. His name was Negro Germán, though he wasn't black except for his tight, curly hair. It seems he had waited for her one day at the entrance of the office building, with a rose."

"Wait, I don't even want to imagine… I'm already feeling secondhand embarrassment."

"Yeah, it was something that stupid. But how do you tell a fool to stop?"

"And what happened in the end?"

"I don't know the details. I only know that the doorman was there with the other employees from the notary's office who had come down to witness this poor devil's cheesy love declaration. She must have said something to him that had the consequences it did. It seems she called him a poor loser or a starving wretch or something like that, because he would have replied that a princess like her might despise a poor loser like him, but deep down that's exactly what snobs like her wanted—a rich guy to marry and a rough guy like him to fuck them good, an uneducated starving wretch to help them endure the marriage. She laughed, and it seems he promised her that one day he'd make her swallow all the milk from his balls. That's when one of the doctor's employees punched him in the face, leaving his mouth bleeding. I don't know if this was before or after he told her he'd make her swallow it all, and with pleasure, but that's more or less how it went."

"A bit over the top, that Germán guy."

"Yeah. But you have to see what a humiliated man is like. The guy quit his job at the notary's office, even though they didn't fire him over the incident, and became a cook at the restaurant on 18 and Ejido."

"*La Pasiva*. The old and beloved La Pasiva."

"That's the one. Now there's a Burger King, but when this happened, it was still the famous La Pasiva. Negro Germán struggled in that job for six months until she showed up with a guy who, in the end, seems to have been the last boyfriend this girl had, a little doctor who works at the American Hospital, though this one doesn't have a BMW."

"You see, doctors aren't what they used to be. Now they're like us."

"She ordered a salad, and he ordered a milanesa napolitana. After all, the little doctor wasn't that much of a snob. Napolitana, not sushi or anything fancy. Then an old waiter from the place served them. When they finished and asked for dessert, Germán went to the bathroom and jerked off as much as he could into a little cup, which he then used to top the chocolate ice cream."

Carlitos made a gesture toward the bar and said:

"Bring me a chocolate ice cream topped with the waiter's cum."

"What a son of a bitch. You're going to make me puke."

When the boyfriend asked for the bill, the guy showed up.

"How was the dessert?" he asked.

She opened her eyes wide, like this. Then the guy asked again:

"Miss, did you enjoy the dessert? It's a house specialty. The secret is in the cream."

"A real son of a bitch, that Germán."

Jacksonville, 2012

The White Coin

When he smelled that metallic scent that always reminded him of his vacations in the mountains, hunting for fun all kinds of small animals that tested their skills to escape by flying, running, or crawling, he imagined Marina calling José Ignacio. His main secretary and his right-hand man had built a special relationship, and he easily guessed the sequence of events. For a moment, he hesitated and smiled.

"Next week," he had told him, delaying without reason the long-awaited promotion. He didn't know why he had done it. He had already decided the kid was worth his weight in gold, and Marina waited day by day, month after month with unspoken expectation for the boss's decision.

Maybe it was a game. He thought that by nature he was somewhat sadistic, a practical man who at every step needed to show his employees that all good things come at a cost. But deep down, as some said, he wasn't that bad. He was fair, terribly fair.

Marina and José Ignacio were the closest thing to what his children would have been. Then he thought about the engineer from the *Tires* division, who had had a child a few days earlier, and he thought that none of his employees had faced hardship in the last ten years, since he decided to restructure the company by firing thirty percent of the staff but saving the rest, who would have been left on the streets if the company had gone bankrupt.

He thought about what the newspapers said about him publicly and what his closest associates said privately: he was a miserly man, not entirely bad, but his greed outweighed any setback or feeling of pity. One of those intellectuals who teach in Europe said that it had been, precisely, greed, the main driving force behind the success of all his companies, and that if any other feeling had taken root in the heart of the famous *entrepreneur*, it surely would have sunk all his enterprises; and with them, the mediocre fate of thousands of highly qualified employees. His only passion, money, had managed to infect, through personal enthusiasm and the example of a model company, a legion of new believers, which is why (he thought, every time he ate, drank, or had sex excessively) one day his death would be widely and uselessly discussed, but it would not end the enduring technological and financial empire he had managed to build from nothing.

He was as proud of himself as he was self-loathing. Over time, he had developed his own psychological theory, despite his intellectual rudiments: every individual who loves themselves for what they do, hates themselves for what they are.

Marina was a girl too young for her talent and sense of responsibility. José Ignacio was not far behind in intelligence and the ability to foresee market demands five years in advance. He shared with him not only a passion for business but also incredibly black eyes, deeply black like the void.

As a child, his grandparents exaggerated their praises and said he looked like an Egyptian statue, silent; with a dark but beautiful gaze, lost in the eternity of the future.

Like his father.

"Why does Clarita have blue eyes and I have black ones, Dad?"

"Because that's how nature is, my little one. Your mom has brown eyes, and I have black eyes. When you were born, you took your mom's red hair and your dad's black eyes. That's why you look a little like both of us."

He was as fascinated by trucks as he was repelled by them. On Saturdays, early in the morning, he would jump for joy when he heard the roar of the Ford. On Sunday nights, he would hide under the sheets to avoid hearing the same rumble that would take his dad away for another week.

Every Saturday, his dad would bring him something new he had gotten on his trucking trips. A miniature car that his school friends took from him; a box of colored pencils; a storybook full of animals and flying Chinese figures; a harmonica that the owner of a boarding house traded for five liters of fuel.

One day, his father couldn't stay until Sunday and had to leave as soon as he arrived. He didn't have time to bring him a gift and gave him a white coin. He remembered perfectly the delicate profile of that woman and his father explaining that with such a shiny coin, he could buy some toy.

As night fell, his father approached the bed and asked him why he was crying.

"I don't want you to leave today," he said.

"I have to do a job at the border, son, I have to go, but I'll be back in a few days."

"You can't go, I don't want you to."

"Look, keep this coin, and next week I'll bring another one, and I promise we'll go to the Turk's store to buy a toy."

"Which one?"

"Any one. With two coins like this, you can buy any toy. So we'll decide when I get back. If you don't lose it, we'll go to the store. During the week, stay with your mom and look in the window for the toy you like the most."

"But the store is closed on Saturday afternoon."

"The Turk will open it for me, I'm sure… Besides, it's possible I'll come back a little earlier this week. Saturday at noon, or maybe Friday afternoon…"

The promise had left him calm but thinking about the next weekend.

His father didn't have dinner before leaving, as usual. He talked with his mother in the kitchen for a long time. Then he listened, with the same anxiety as every Sunday, to the preparations for the trip and the roar of the truck that gradually faded among the noise of the engines of others like it driving down the street.

Late at night, they arrived.

His mother said he wasn't there.

"Don't lie, ma'am, we know he's hiding somewhere in the house."

They searched, fruitlessly and with growing frustration, the entire house. When one of them approached him, he asked what he was hiding in his hand. He didn't answer. Then one of them grabbed his hand and forced it open until the white coin fell out.

"Well, well," said the other. "What are we going to do with so much money?"

He ran to grab it, but one of them was faster and took it from him.

"What's your name?"

He didn't respond.

"Did the mice eat your tongue? Well, if you don't answer me, you won't get your money back."

He remembers screaming in desperation and someone grabbing him by the shoulders as if they were a pair of pliers.

"Again. What's your name?"

"Alejandro," he said.

"Well, what a nice name. And your dad?"

He didn't get an answer.

"If you don't tell me your dad's name, I won't give you your coin back."

"Ernesto."

"Well, what a nice name. Ernesto…. And where is Ernesto?"

"I don't know."

"But how, how can a son not know where his father is? Doesn't your father love you?"

"Yes."

"Then, where's your daddy?"

No answer.

"Very well. We'll have to take the coin."

"No! The coin, no…"

"Do you want your little coin? Yes? No? Yes… Then, tell us where your daddy is. We need to pay him for a job.

"In the truck. He went to the border."

He remembered his mother's desperate cry, saying *no*, that he had gone to Sierra, to Sierra del Rio.

"To the border, Mom. Dad told me he was going to the border."

And his mother, shouting even louder, saying no, that he had gone to Sierra del Rio, as always.

"Good boy," said one of them. "Here's your coin."

Alejandro took the white coin and clenched it tightly, remembering his father's smile when he last said "next week," and he fired.

Jacksonville, 2013

The yellow house

SOSA WAS WORRIED about his son, Edison, since he turned nine. He had started looking for his own features in the boy's face and had come to the conclusion that, without a doubt, he was his son.

But the boy cried more often than usual, still wet the bed after a couple of corrections, at school he preferred to sit next to a girl, and during recess he recited Martí's verses, which the teacher had assigned as homework, instead of playing cops and robbers with the other boys. At fourteen, Edison showed an inclination for music, more specifically for the piano, and at fifteen he came home one day saying, with enthusiasm as if he had won a prize, that the *high school* teacher had seen good potential in him for classical dance.

At eighteen, Mr. Sosa enrolled Edison in the *army*, which also had the advantage of paying for his college education.

That same year, as his father had done in Puerto Rico, he took him to a brothel in Daytona. But the madam who ran the place noticed that Edison seemed underage.

"How old is the boy?" she asked.

Sosa wasn't exactly sure what age marked the start of adulthood in his country, which still felt foreign to him. He cut to the chase and answered:

"Twenty-one."

"Of course he's not twenty-one," said the woman. "Do you think I was born yesterday? I've been sucking on something else for forty years, and I know when daddies bring their little boys to us to make them men. I've eaten up more than one boy like this, and I can recognize one who's just lost his baby teeth."

"Nineteen. Fine, he's nineteen," said Sosa.

"Not twenty-one, not nineteen. The boy's barely sixteen. What do you want me to do with one of my girls? He's got nothing to work with. Wait until he becomes a real man before bringing him back."

"I'm eighteen," said Edison, momentarily snapping out of the terror the idea of making a fool of himself in front of a naked woman had caused him, "and I do have what it takes, I've got enough to give and share with any of those whores and you too, with all the rides you've got on your record."

"Don't make me laugh, little baby. Finish your milk and then we'll talk. And you, sir, out of respect for having once been one of my clients, if I recall correctly, I ask you to take this chick out of here. I don't want to have any more trouble with the police, understand? And because I know you, I know you're not one of those camouflaged types, but I don't want to risk anything. I want to retire soon."

Sosa, smiling to ease the tension of the situation, asked for an exception for the boy until the madam threatened to call the police. Sosa burst out laughing. He knew that more than one of the girls was illegal in several ways, but he didn't want to push it. Edison had turned pale and seemed to be trembling, if not from fear then at least from anger. That's where he took after his father, he thought, hard to control.

On the way home, Edison didn't say a word. He just listened to his father's fragmented monologue, congratulating him on his intervention (those whores deserved nothing less) but also pointing out other flaws, like how he had chickened out in the end, "like a wet little chick," he said.

Edison would forever remember the face of the woman they called "the Colombian," her tired eyes with wrinkles, her straw-blonde dyed hair, and her full lips that weren't entirely sensual. Those red lips that had spat in his face, "you've got nothing to work with," like a confirmation of what he had always suspected. He wasn't man enough for women who knew what it was like to be taken by real beasts of burden.

The following Saturday, he decided to put an end to all the plans and speculations that had tormented him during the week and asked his father for the car.

"You're in luck," said Sosa, "because I'm beat and I'm not going out tonight."

When he handed him the keys to the old Buick, he warned him:

"Drive carefully. And be careful who you bring into the car. You know, like *watermelons*, they have to be ready to split. Always check if the girl has a pit in her throat; it's like the lack of hips or a deep voice…"

"I'm going to the beach with friends, Dad."

"Yeah, I used to say the same thing back in San Juan."

Edison returned to the Colombian's brothel. But as he parked, he saw a group of Mexicans entering, joking around, and he thought his Plan A was either crazy or simply beyond his capabilities. He was going to make a fool of himself once again, and he knew he wouldn't be able to recover from another defeat.

So he went with Plan B. He sped down the beach at sixty miles per hour, entered Daytona to the south, and in one of the darkest areas of Port Orange, around eleven P.M., he arrived at an address he had tracked online. It appeared in various forums where dozens of anonymous users praised or mocked the old women of Casa Amarilla.

He put the GPS in the glove compartment and took out a plastic gun, which he hid in his jacket. The night and the silence amplified the salty smell of the sea. That sense of unreality dulled any rational thought and carried him like a wave toward his destination.

Plan B turned out to be simpler than expected, as soon as he crossed the threshold. It was indeed a brothel. The house was organized like the Hispanic homes of the past: a central courtyard surrounded by arches that during the day protected the hallway from the sun and at that hour cast black shadows over the doors where the women of the night waited. The *women of the night*, as his father called them.

The moonlight fell on the face of a young woman who smiled at him, but by that point Edison had no clear idea of what he was doing, so he kept walking as if he knew what he was about. He settled on the second face that smiled at him, this time from a curved shadow.

The second face wasn't as beautiful, or it belonged to a woman in her forties, maybe fifties, but it inspired more confidence in him. Beauty intimidated him to the point of paralysis. He placed a hand on her cheek, and the woman took his arm. She smiled, said, "Good evening, welcome."

Without looking at him, with movements Edison guessed were routine in her profession, the woman headed to the bathroom while asking, "Where have you been all this time, dear?"

Edison didn't answer. It was obviously another stock phrase, part of the trade. He saw her buttocks, quite firm for her age, her breasts slightly sagging after being freed from her bra. He thought about his own body, which hadn't yet responded to the situation as it should have.

The woman had to make an effort to put the client at ease so he could relieve himself in the usual fifteen minutes. A television lit her face in red and blue, advertising the exchange of an old car for the new *Ford* 2009. Don Francisco insisted that Ramiro, from San Salvador, kneel before his wife to ask for forgiveness for being unfaithful. His wife forgave him, and the audience erupted with emotion. A close-up captured a face in the audience, bathed in tears.

"*Very well done, sir. Thank you very much. Our secretaries will take you through the Tunnel of Love, where our Latin Queen awaits to present you with two cruise tickets to the Virgin Islands and Barbados. In our next block, sponsored by Big Shield, 'insure, insure me before it's too late,' we'll have the children from the panel who will give us advice on marriage and much more, on Saaaaaaaabado Gigante...*"

Almost at the end, Edison managed to focus and fulfill his duty as a man. He saw the woman's breasts, large, heaving but sagging, her eyes open toward the ceiling, as if she were suffering while repeating that he was doing very well, that it was almost over, that he was almost there. Finally, he let out a half-hearted cry.

The woman gave him five extra minutes. Edison wanted to know something about the woman who had been his first, the one who had made him a man. He learned she was Cuban, that life here hadn't been as easy as she had imagined on the island. She had been the queen of Camagüey and had been told that with her beauty, she would become the Latin Queen in Miami. But a stupid jury failed to appreciate her pride for having crossed that shark-infested sea to show the world what it means to be a true queen, a condition that isn't inherited but carried in the blood, and they accused her of arrogance, and she was never able to fulfill her true destiny.

Edison, who had introduced himself as Ignacio from the start, was about to ask her how she had ended up there, but he realized that Laira must have heard the same question a thousand times and that she would have always repeated the same lie in response. He also thought the story of being the queen of Camagüey was false. He had met many other immigrants who exaggerated their merits; even they had convinced themselves of their own fantasies.

The following Saturday, Edison returned to Casa Amarilla. He never saw the yellow color of its walls, despite the intense brightness of the moon, perhaps, he thought, because that color is one of the first to fade in the darkness.

He looked for Laira. No one knew her. He thought it was a made-up name, that maybe the Cuban woman invented a different name every night, which is why her companions couldn't identify her. To one woman, who invited him in, he explained that she was Cuban.

"In the house, there are three Cubans, two Venezuelans, one Argentine, and one American. You can't complain, boy, you've got options."

"The Cuban I'm looking for is a redhead, older than you…"

"Look, chick, I think she's not here, and she's not a redhead."

"What's her name?"

"Oh no, boy, we don't give out personal information here. Make do with what's available or move on."

Edison left but returned the following Monday and Tuesday until he began to attract the attention of the women in the house.

Almost a month later, on a Friday, after three hours of patient waiting in his car, he saw her arrive. He waited half an hour and went in. Laira, or whatever her name was, was in her usual spot. Edison smiled at her:

"Hi, Laira. How are you?"

Laira didn't respond. Her face revealed surprise and terror. She stepped back and said she wasn't available. She tried to close the door, but Edison put his hand in the way. The door squeezed his fingers, and Laira begged him to please remove his hand or he would get hurt. Almost murmuring, Edison said to her:

"You're hurting me, Laira. You're breaking my fingers."

"Go, please, leave. That's it. I'm telling you I'm not working today."

"Why are you lying to me, Laira?"

"My name isn't Laira, and now leave me alone or I'll call the police."

"What's wrong, Laira, didn't you like it last time? Do I seem so insignificant to you? Do you want me to pay you more? I have money. Why are you crying? You're crushing my fingers."

Laira gave in, and Edison, with a push, managed to get inside. He threw her onto the bed and unzipped his pants.

"I'll scream, and the other girls will come. Please, don't be foolish," said Laira.

Edison threw himself on Laira, and Laira began to scream.

In an instant, one of the women from the house rushed in and lunged at Edison, throwing him to the floor. But Edison got up and slapped her. The woman responded by grabbing his hair. Hysterical, she screamed, "abuser, abuser." Until she slowly fell, sliding down Edison's body.

Edison had pulled out a knife that pierced the Argentine woman's abdomen, and when he realized what he had done, he was petrified with horror. The Argentine woman was already dead when Laira took Edison by the arm and said to him:

"Leave, Edison, leave now, before the police come."

Edison looked at her in astonishment. He was a second away from asking her how she knew his name.

Finally, he fled. On the beach, the Buick hit a wave and flipped several times. Edison partially lost his sight and sense of smell. Thanks to a precise surgical intervention, he was able to regain his sight, but he could never again smell the salty sea.

Laira confirmed in her statement that Edison was a bit drunk, had wanted to have relations with her, and she had refused because she knew Edison was the son she had given up almost twenty years ago to the good man Sosa, who believed he was his son and never dared or wanted to confirm it. Laira began to scream, and Raquel, the Argentine woman, had come to her aid. But in the struggle, Lilian, whom Edison knew as Laira, had accidentally hurt Raquel with the knife she always kept in her nightstand, more to scare off violent men than for anything else.

Jacksonville, 2014

Life is like that

Dad, we need to talk. I know it will be hard for you to hear what I have to say, but I also know that you'll learn to accept it over time…

Your wife and I are going to separate. Both of us are going to form new families. You will come with me and live with Amalia. Amalia is the mom I met at daycare. Remember that lady with black hair who always went with a blond boy who wore glasses? Well, that's her. It wasn't love at first sight. It was something that developed over time. I don't know how to explain it to you.

I know that right now you're probably thinking, "How is it possible for a daughter to stop loving one mother and start loving another?" But there are things, feelings that we children have that an adult could never understand. Surely when you're an old man, you'll manage to understand it. Old people remember their childhood better than the rest of their lives, marked by confusion and the fantasies of adults. That's why I ask you not to try to understand everything. Just accept it as it is, since it's a decision that's been made. The longer you take, the more you'll suffer.

Amalia has a five-year-old son from before, almost the same age as me, so I'm sure that you'll learn to love him as Mom will learn to love Ignacio's girl, as if she were me.

We've already talked about it with your wife. Sometimes the relationship between a child and one of their parents doesn't work out, and the best thing, to avoid conflicts that harm both, is separation.

You know that things between Mom and I haven't been good for a long time. Once, she even spanked me because I spilled coffee on her computer. That damn computer that destroyed our mother-daughter relationship. I didn't report it to the school teacher to avoid taking things to an extreme that could harm her even more.

The spankings, that primitive reaction, typical of caveman parents, were just the last straw. We decided to separate on good terms. Yes, I know you love your wife, but you'll learn to live without her and to love Amalia as you love Mom. She'll also have to get used to the new husband she got by chance, Carmencita's dad, a good man, they say, and he'll also learn to love and respect her as you did. You'll be able to visit her on weekends.

I know it's not the best, but the truth is that there's no middle ground. I can't live with your wife anymore, and you can't live with her and me under the same roof. Imagine her having to cross paths every morning with my new mother and me having to see her new children hugging her and covering her with kisses, and her happily fulfilled as a mother. Deep down, I couldn't stand it either, no matter how fair it is.

No, it's also not possible to have a third house where you and Mom can live alone. I need a father, and you need me too. When I turn eighteen, then you'll be free and can go back to Mom if you want. I'm still a child, and I have the right to rebuild my life. You, on the other hand, are an adult, you've already lived a big part of your life, you have experience, and this change won't traumatize you. You'll learn to accept it over time.

You will also have to be a understanding and thoughtful father. Amalia has her flaws and virtues, but she is a good woman and a good mother. She's not great in the kitchen, so I hope you learn to cook for the four of us, and when she does cook, have the tact to praise her effort.

I know this takes you a bit by surprise, though you must have guessed it for some time now. I know it's not easy to have to live with and love another mother as you loved your wife. But it's not about replacing your feelings. You will continue to love your wife as always, only now you'll have to learn to live with another woman and do your best to love her as I love her.

Imagine how absurd it would be if it had been you, the father, who decided to leave with another woman, and I, the child, who had to face the unexpected blow and take on the responsibility and obligation to adapt to such a problem, an adult problem, one of those sudden and unpredictable whims typical of adults? I would have to force myself to love the new mom you chose. Obviously, I couldn't handle it, because I'm a very young child. But you are an adult, and you will know how to adapt and respect the emotions and feelings of a young child. Of course, that kind of thing happened in the savage societies of your great-grandparents, but fortunately, today we children have our rights secured. We are no longer little woolen sacks where adults dump all their whims and frustrations. It will be my turn when I'm an adult to protect my children from my loves and heartbreaks.

I know it hurts, that your old heart will struggle to accept it, but there's no turning back. You will have to learn to love Amalia as I will learn to love Pablito as if he were my brother. In fact, he will be my brother from today on. You'll see that Amalia is also a charming wife… What can you do, Dad. Don't cry. Life is like that.

Ewing, 2009

The Last Step

When he opened his eyes he saw her face in the darkness. It was the ghost of María. He said her name, trying to verify what couldn't be real: María had died a year ago.

"It's me…"

"María?"

"No, Ernesto. Mom died a long time ago. It's me, Lucía."

He made a great effort to recognize Lucía in that face. But the ghost of María persisted in Lucía, who, between laughter and tears, repeated his name: Ernesto, finally, Ernesto…

Ernesto was still drunk, not understanding. He barely remembered the events of the previous day. The argument in the kitchen. Lucía going up the stairs to the bedroom and him following behind. He was reproaching her for something Lucía didn't want to hear. What was he trying to tell her? He couldn't remember.

"Ernesto, finally, Ernesto…"

Ernesto had gone up the stairs but must have had too much to drink, because no matter how hard he tried, he couldn't reach the last steps. The urge to cry without crying, the urge to scream in pain without saying anything.

Then, yes(he remembered it perfectly, like a vertigo), he had fallen backward and into the void.

That had happened fourteen years ago. In between, nothing, not the slightest dream, not a single memory, not a word of hope or comfort, none of all those things his son Gustavo had repeated to him so often in the early years, before all his transformations and long before avoiding the living tomb of his father.

Lucía had become the living image of her mother. But Ernesto could still see in many details that distinguished her from her parents (the sometimes affectionate gaze, the posture of her full lips) those signs of the tender and passionate love of their early years together.

The world and his family had changed, as always, in unexpected ways. Lucía had not only aged fourteen years in the blink of an eye; the little Gustavo he had seen yesterday at five years old had just been expelled from university for drug use on campus. The cheerful and restless boy now had thick, darker hair, a lost gaze, and confused speech. The worst: his son couldn't manage to show any emotion, good or bad, toward the people around him. His most frequent responses were "yes" and "no," which to the convalescing Ernesto sounded like "I don't know, I have no idea" or "I'm not interested." His drowsy face was always lit up by the cell phone he checked incessantly, even though he no longer had a girlfriend and almost no friends.

Ernesto had to make an even greater effort than with Lucía to recognize in that tall, thin young man, in that man, his son. By the magic of a simple blow, the father had not only missed his son's childhood and adolescence, his past, but also his future. Gustavo had also lost his own future, that future full of promise that the healthy five-year-old boy had deserved. Five years earlier, he had contracted AIDS as soon as he began experimenting with drugs.

Lucía was also reluctant to engage in conversation. She said that this impression was due to his physical and emotional state. A person who has spent fourteen years in a coma doesn't recover overnight. Not only had his muscles suffered from inactivity, but the world had become something unrecognizable to someone who hadn't accompanied it through all its changes.

Quickly, Ernesto felt nostalgia for the previous day, just after waking from the coma. The first hours had been confusing for him, but joyful for Lucía and the nurses. The doctor had called Lucía because he had detected changes in his condition, and her face was the second face he saw before understanding what had happened. But as the days passed, things began to change. Lucía's joy and Gustavo's forced smile began to lose their resolve. For Gustavo, the man who had awakened was no longer his father. For Lucía, he had ceased to be her husband.

Over time, the desire for Ernesto to wake up turned into resentment. Mother and son had barely survived. They had learned to live without him. They had even learned to live with a father who was neither alive nor dead, which was worse than being alive or dead.

He had to listen, with remorse, to every detail of how Gustavo had contracted the AIDS virus from his cocaine-addicted friends or as a result of a bad tattoo, a skull with a crown of roses and inscriptions in Chinese and Hebrew that he couldn't even read. In high school, he had never been a good student, but his hell had begun with the tattoos and the addiction, not just to cocaine but to a very limited number of things and activities, like checking his cell phone or practicing *skateboarding* until he fractured his elbows and ankles. He had lasted a little longer in university than in any job, thanks to various psychological support programs that he eventually abandoned.

Lucía had managed to carry on with her life and her son's, who insisted on blaming her for all his misfortunes, including his father's, with the emotional and financial support of a man with whom, just a few days earlier, she had decided to move in permanently. She couldn't sell the house, nor could she live with him there. So she planned to leave it to Gustavo, who saw this change as the beginning of his illusory liberation. Now the father's return complicated things as much as his absence had.

All of it, Ernesto told himself in the solitude of the night, because of one too many drinks.

Five days later, one night in the kitchen of the Charleston house, at Ernesto's insistence, Lucía recounted the accident and the circumstances that had caused it. One summer, Ernesto had developed a habit of drinking heavily and would get irritated over anything. (Why? She didn't know, things weren't that bad between them, his work at the hospital was excellent.) One night, Lucía reproached him for the bad example he was setting for their son, they argued, and she retreated to the upstairs bedroom. He went up the stairs and, before reaching the last step, fell backward.

Ernesto remembered this last part, especially the difficulty he felt in reaching the last step first and then grabbing the handrail. Then that vertigo he had dreamed of several times after the coma.

Lucía stared at him as if studying his face.

"Don't you remember anything else?" she asked.

"No," Ernesto replied. "I don't remember anything after that."

"And before?"

"Not that either. Should I remember something important?"

"No," Lucía answered. "I just want you to recover."

In truth, Ernesto felt tired but remembered many things, like a normal person waking up from a deep night's rest.

One day, Ernesto told Lucía that he had some fragmented memories. He lied, saying he was beginning to remember the argument that had led him to the stairs.

"We were arguing about another man…" Ernesto said, as if lost in thought.

"No," Lucía quickly replied. "Don't form false memories. We were arguing because our relationship had deteriorated a lot, and you had made up that story about another man. There was never another man until…"

"Until when?"

"Until long after you fell into a coma." The life insurance ran out in less than three years, and with my job at Barnes & Noble, I could barely pay the bills…

"So it was out of necessity,"

"No… If it had been out of necessity, I would have found another man much sooner."

"Well, at least you fell in love seriously once."

"You haven't changed at all. Of course, fourteen years haven't passed for you. You're still the same. Anyway, yes, I did fall in love, but not for the first time. The first time was in Philadelphia. I was sixteen. A nearly platonic love, if you don't count the kisses in Franklin Square. The second time I fell in love seriously. I don't know if you heard. It was in college."

"But that love died. Maybe when Gustavo was born, who knows, right?"

"Yes, who knows. But I know that love didn't die; we killed it little by little."

"I have the feeling we've had this same conversation before."

"It's not just a feeling. We've had this same conversation many times, and every time we ended up arguing."

"Maybe that love didn't die; it turned into a horrible monster..."

"It's getting late," she said, picking up her purse.

Ernesto gave up trying to remember along these paths. He still loved that woman (he almost told her), now gaunt and filled with sadness, but he couldn't tell if he still loved her as he had the first time. Maybe that was the central problem: pretending that things could stay the same despite the passage of time, without learning to recognize and appreciate those very changes, the different forms love took to renew itself, to stay alive.

Surely she didn't suffer from these complexities. She had once told him that she was the masculine side of the house and he the feminine side: she passionate, simple, and practical; he complicated and sentimental, obsessed with romantic love, which, by definition, is the flower of a few days.

While he was recovering, she would visit him in the afternoons and leave promptly at seven in the evening. Once she told him that the other man—Ernesto didn't know his name; he didn't need to, because Gustavo would stay to live with him—contrary to what he believed, wasn't sad about his waking from the coma. Now she could free herself from his ghost definitively. She could also get a divorce to live a normal life.

Then Ernesto remembered that this had been another recurring topic of argument. She had asked him for a divorce more than once, and he had avoided answering, saying he needed time to think about it. The truth, which even he couldn't see clearly, was that he still loved Lucía with a sick obsession.

One night, he asked her if they had a wedding date yet, and she replied that it wasn't his problem. The only thing he had to do was file for divorce. He didn't answer, which she interpreted as a threat. She managed to break Ernesto's silence in an argument that escalated quickly.

"You've started drinking again," she reproached him.

"No more than you. Do you feel bad? Yes? Because I'm still very lucid…"

"You're the same cynic as always," said Lucía, and she left the kitchen.

She went up the stairs to the bedroom. Ernesto followed her. She was on the last step. He remembered those eyes, hard as marble, waiting for him on the last step. And he remembered that as they struggled, he, intoxicated by alcohol and jealousy, wanted to tell her that he loved her, that he loved her like a teenager and almost like a child. Neither had he known how to love her, or he loved her like a sick madman. And both of them were sick, or that passionate, romantic love that Ernesto had invented had made them sick.

But he was surprised by her hand, pushing him by the shoulder. He tried to resist, like in a child's nightmare, when he dreamed of falling into the void. In that instant, he knew the pain he felt was for her. And for her, he had forgotten that hand that fourteen years earlier had prevented him from reaching the last step first and the handrail afterward.

But Ernesto didn't move forward. He was still weak and became breathless at the slightest effort. He managed to stop halfway and think for a moment.

Then he went back down to the kitchen and sat down again next to the glass of wine. He saw her hurry past and leave quickly through the front door.

The next day, the medical examiner confirmed that Ernesto had died from the injuries sustained in the fall down the stairs. His blood showed a very high level of alcohol.

Newark, 2008

Bad Move

Lupita was always a child forced to grow up through hardship. But even then, she never matured, and I didn't want her to. She was so lovely and affectionate just the way she was. All her childhood of hunger and her adolescence of shouting and humiliation hadn't made her tougher, more resistant to the lot life had dealt her—quite the opposite. To me, the old man treated her so badly because Lupita's mother had died in childbirth, and he never forgave her for it.

Who knows if she would have survived the streets of the slum where I took her to save her from the old man's alcoholism. Who knows if she would have had a better life among the subways of New York. Who knows if she would have come if I hadn't painted her a picture of gold and glory on the other side. Don't suffer anymore, Lupita, you can't live like this, half in tears. I'm off to Yankee-land, and whatever happens, happens. After all, who's going to know we have a picture of Che in the kitchen? We'll take it down tomorrow and put on our best smiles at the embassy.

"They're not going to give a visa to two poor folks like us, Nacho. We don't even have enough to eat."

"No one knows that, not your father, not your sister. Least of all my poor old mother, who's half-blind. You'll follow me later."

"I can't stand the thought of you leaving," she'd tell me, and I'd say we wouldn't be apart for long.

"How long isn't long? A year? Two years?"

"No, not that long. Just a few months. As soon as I can save up for your plane ticket, you'll come."

Back then, they didn't deny visas like they do now. Besides, Lupita had a translator's degree, though in the two years we lived together in the slum, she only got paid for one job because I had to go in person to throw my weight around. And after they stole our TV and the Teflon pots Lupita's sister had given us—luckily we weren't in the shack that Saturday—I told her I was leaving in February.

We spent the whole Sunday staring at the ceiling, watching the zinc sheets sweat from the sheer humid heat that wouldn't let us sleep. But it wasn't the heat, it was this life we'd been dealt, and there was no man strong enough to bend it, and if I'd known, I wouldn't have come into this world under these conditions.

"And when are we going to have a child like that?" she'd start, and I'd say nothing, absolutely nothing, because I had nothing to say. I thought that if she hadn't been so miserable with her father, I'd never have taken her from her house. At least there they had a ceiling and the neighbor's dog barking at her from the rooftop, and the roof didn't sweat in the summer, and there was no shortage of bread and pasta on Sundays, and the sad stories from the old Italian man before the heat of the sauce and the fumes of the red wine went to his head. Sure, there were plenty of fights and shouting, but damn those people. 'Dad, have some coffee, please, Dad, Nacho's here today.' 'What Nacho? Don't tell me what to do in my own house, have you ever seen such a thing? Make coffee for your man, see if he doesn't run off, and I'll have to put up with another slacker like this one.' 'Another what, Dad? I've only had two boyfriends.' 'Look, don't make me talk. Why, Don Paolo? What do you have to say that I don't know?' 'Two that I know of,' the old man would say, and he'd start getting worked up. And me, with my macho complex, wanted to know how many boyfriends Lupita had had. 'Lupita's no saint. About ten, or eleven, the whole neighborhood soccer team.' 'Don't say that, Dad, you know it's not true, don't be mean.' 'Mean? I didn't even count the substitutes.' And then I'd bring up Lupita's acknowledged ex-boyfriend, and she'd defend herself by saying I knew she was a virgin when we met and other things that aren't even worth bringing up now."

"The heart is blind," I'd tell Lupita. "Otherwise, the eyes wouldn't be in the head; they'd be in the heart. If I hadn't fallen in love, I wouldn't have left my mother's house either. But there are things you can't choose. I fell in love, and I could never stop loving Lupita, like a sick man, I couldn't."

I'd think about all that, staring at the sweaty ceiling, and I wasn't getting anywhere. Then she'd get sadder because I didn't want to talk. But I never stopped thinking and thinking. That's what I remember most from that time. I spent my days thinking, calculating, imagining, fantasizing for nothing.

Until last February, when the club's youth team made the long-awaited tour of Los Angeles, and one night there, after the game we tied two-two, with a terrible performance from my left wing, I disappeared. I left the pit, as the guys from school used to say. They say the coach looked for me but didn't get too worked up about it. Besides, he knew I was a hack and had no future in the club. Not in that one or any other. And since I wasn't Cuban, no one even noticed. After that, I stayed quiet when a Mexican guy gave me a gig at his restaurant in Santa Monica.

It took me two days to find a job, and Lupita wrote to me saying how wonderful it was, how wonderful, Nacho, now we'll finally be able to live our lives in peace.

For me, at first, it was paradise. Reading Lupita's emails, so happy despite not sleeping at night because of the fear in the slum. But she had so much hope and kept talking about the child we didn't have yet, saying we shouldn't be negative for now, that things worked better that way. So I exaggerated all the good things here or didn't mention that one day I'd run into a gang, a "patota" as they call it back home, and had to hand over all the money I'd earned that week. "Don't open your mouth," a

Panamanian friend told me. "They'll mistake you for an American because of your hair and eyes, but as soon as you say something, they'll figure out you're illegal, that you're paid in cash, and they'll follow you and leave you without a dollar, in the best-case scenario."

But little by little, everything changed. In two months, I'd saved enough for Lupita's ticket, but then the crisis hit, and I was the first to go before the restaurant closed because I was the new guy, they said. Still, I sent the money to Lupita so she could come, because we couldn't take it anymore. I didn't think it would be so hard to find work after that.

With Lupita, we searched in Los Angeles, then in Las Vegas, and then all over Arizona until we ended up in San Antonio, with a promise from a Puerto Rican guy who had a cleaning business. The truth is, cleaning hotels and offices wasn't as easy as it seemed at first. The boss was always unhappy with our work. If it wasn't too slow, it was too careless. I started to think he was messing with us, or maybe we just didn't understand what he wanted, and two weeks later, we were back on the street.

Literally on the street, because we had to wait on a corner in the early morning hours where they picked up undocumented workers. And there I was with Lupita, surrounded by men who, luckily, didn't treat us badly—quite the opposite—but the truth is, I always had Jesus on my lips and was looking everywhere to see who might mess with Lupita. So much so that I wasn't paying attention to the trucks that passed by picking up workers. The Mexicans were the most skilled at this, and I had to watch and learn from them. Sometimes Lupita would ask why I didn't approach the guy in the white truck, the one in the black car who seemed to have good work, but the truth is, I didn't want to leave her there alone, waiting, before it was fully light, so I'd pretend to be distracted or say that one wasn't right for us for this or that reason.

Until a black SUV passed by and signaled to one of the men, who came over to tell me they wanted the girl. I went up to the truck, and the guy with sunglasses at that hour didn't inspire much confidence. He said he had work for housekeepers in a wealthy family's home, but I didn't see any other women in the back. Lupita, paler than usual and with trembling lips, told me we couldn't let this one slip by because we wouldn't have enough to eat.

I didn't say anything, but she ended up getting in the back, surely against her own will. And when the truck started moving, she waved her little hand at me and blew me a sad kiss. I knew she was crying because I know her. I knew this wasn't going to work, and this damn life wasn't going to work either.

Philadelphia, 2009

The Last Summer

Just imagining the loneliness of a coffin gives me claustrophobia," said Camilo, leaning his head back and burying his feet in the sand.

The sun made him close his eyes.

"Don't be ridiculous," she said, with an unconvincing smile. "Why are you thinking about those things now?"

"Nothing. I was thinking about my retirement. I'd like to move to Florida when there's nothing important left to do. Then old age and all that came to mind. Sooner or later, it'll be a reality, won't it?"

"What does that matter? When the time comes, you won't even notice. You could make an effort not to ruin the vacation."

"What if I wake up in the middle of the night like it's happened to so many people? I've often dreamed something like that and woken up suffocating."

"As you always say, it's logical, isn't it?"

"What's logical?"

"If you felt suffocated for any other reason, it's logical that you'd dream about situations like that."

"Ah, very good. Ten more years of marriage, and you'll leave painting for the stock market."

"God forbid!"

"Don't say that, that's how we make a living. One bad decision, and we wouldn't be here." Another one, and we won't have the retirement you're imagining for twenty years from now.

* * *

The doctor had the envelope open. He took out a sheet of paper and put it back. He removed his glasses, and Camilo saw his tired eyes.

"Any news, doctor?"

The doctor didn't answer. He adjusted himself in his chair and took the paper out of the envelope again. He put on his glasses and read.

"Is something wrong, doctor?"

"We need to run more tests."

"Did these come back bad?"

"No…"

"But…? I feel perfectly fine… is there a problem?"

"Life is a problem that needs to be solved."

"I'm serious, doctor. I'm not paying you to philosophize."

"Yes, yes, don't worry."

"I am worried. I'm worried because when someone feels fine and a doctor isn't so sure, it's because something serious must be going on. Tell me straight, did the tests come back bad."

"No... I mean, yes. These tests aren't entirely conclusive."

"Conclusive? Conclusive for what? Do I have something serious?"

"We don't know yet. We need to run more blood tests."

* * *

Ever since he found out he would die soon, he stopped caressing her the way he always had. After a week, Hannah began to worry. But she hid it. At first, because these mood swings in Camilo weren't unusual. Always worried about everything, as if the fate of the world depended on what he did or didn't do.

Then, she began to suspect that his skills as a lover had declined just as Camilo's energy had declined from overwork or from a progressive sadness that had caught him at forty, just like his mother.

There she was, lying on the bed, on her side, enjoying one of those moments of deep sleep. Camilo looked at the profile of her shoulder, the curve from her abdomen to her hips, gently undulating with her breathing. He looked at that bare back he had caressed in so many ways and couldn't remember when the passion of the early years had turned into that deep love that had no shape or name.

The cool breeze of a summer that was slow to leave occasionally moved the papers Hannah had piled on her desk.

She put so much love into her drawings, he thought. If she put more passion and less love, she'd be a recognized artist. Gloria, the only gallery owner who had shown interest in her, would respect her more than the money he discreetly sent to the gallery in the form of donations. Yes, Hannah loved more than she desired. That was the explanation for her failure, he thought.

"Hannah...," he said almost in a whisper.

He wasn't calling her. He was calling himself. An instinctive movement led him to wrap an arm around her, but he held back. Now more than ever, he had to rely without exception on the virtues that had characterized him over the last ten years. Virtues? No, flaws, as she said when she got furious. That obsession with always going for the practical, calculating losses and gains in every decision without putting his heart into it, without ever shedding a sentimental tear. That sick rationalism, Hannah said when she was angry, that doesn't speak just to speak or argue just to argue if it doesn't solve the problem.

"Almost all of a woman's body is sex," thought Camilo, as he tasted something salty in his mouth, as if he were still in the Keys. "The same goes for a man's brain. Almost all of a man's brain, at least a young man's, is sex. They're more romantic, we're more pornographic. That's why they get lost in a maze of inconsistencies, and we're mortally more practical."

Ernesto had once told him that his pragmatism was leaking somewhere, because he didn't consider that a woman doesn't need him to solve the problems she invents as substitutes for the real problems she has.

"So you're saying that when Hannah comes to me with a problem and I solve it, I'm doing wrong?"

"Correct."

"Please, I have enough problems as it is without having to guess that a complaint about the misuse of time is actually about the misuse of my patience to listen to the complaint about the misuse of time."

"Well, that's your problem. I never understood how an artist like Hannah ended up marrying a relentless businessman like you."

"Neither did I. But it's worked out pretty well."

"It's worked, but if you'd calculated better, you never would've married her. Or am I wrong?"

Many times Camilo had secretly promised himself to change. He didn't want to admit it, but he had tried. And he had always failed.

The logic of things was always superior, and he couldn't lie to himself.

* * *

In the elevator, he ran into Ms. Robinson. He smiled at her. She responded as always, with her automatic, unfriendly gesture.

"Hi," she said.

Camilo raised his eyebrows.

"Good morning," he replied, distant.

"A bad one?" she asked.

"Why do you say that?"

"I'm sorry. Just a silly comment."

When the door opened, Ms. Robinson hurried out. Camilo stood pensive and had to quickly put his hand out to keep the elevator from closing again.

* * *

It must have been a coincidence. That night, Ms. Robinson returned shortly before Camilo. Camilo stalled by checking his pockets. He went back to the car. He checked a ticket. He didn't read it. He returned to the entrance. She didn't open the first door for him. He opened the second one without saying a word.

In the elevator, two floors up, their eyes met. Camilo noticed that Ms. Robinson had dark eyes. Ms. Robinson held his gaze for a second. Maybe two seconds, long enough for an unexpected complicity to form.

Someone had scratched the button panel with something sharp. The beep sounded three times at each floor.

Ms. Robinson's purse was green. Her perfume grew stronger as she left.

Before the summer ended, Ms. Robinson had shown him, for the first time in his life, the vertigo of the forbidden. The torment of guilt he already knew, and it didn't even console him to think he was acting correctly, according to a plan.

* * *

After almost a month of barely speaking to her, of sleeping on the living room couch, he realized he had miscalculated. In the end, he hadn't managed to earn Hannah's contempt, and now he felt there had never been a need to destroy their marriage to save her.

The night before, he went to the bedroom and slipped into her bed. She didn't wake up until he hugged her from behind. A moment later, he heard her breathing and a whimper that was like a stifled laugh. He ran a hand over her face and her eyes. His hand felt that they were crying.

* * *

He took Camilo's cell phone and placed it in his hand against his chest.

The funeral home employees exchanged glances and, after a few seconds, closed the coffin.

That night, she dialed his number. It rang a couple of times, three times, and she hung up. She called again at midnight. She didn't wait long and hung up again. At 3:35 in the morning, she called one last time.

Camilo's voice answered for him:

"Hello, I can't take your call right now. If you think something in this life has no solution, you've called the right number. We can help you. Please leave your message, and I'll return your call as soon as possible. Thank you…"

Jacksonville, 2011

Apocryphal Roman

AT THE EDGE OF THE EMPIRE and the world, an old man lamented day and night, waiting uselessly for death. As he waited, he told this story to those who dared to venture there:

I have discovered that in the depths of the Empire, my name is cursed. To pursue those who remember me this way would be futile and would only increase the sad fame that will prolong my shadow until the end of time. They will remember me for a single day, extinguished forever in Palestine.

When the protests began (not against my government or the Empire, but against one man), I didn't think about the gravity of such an insignificant event. I knew that Caesar would only care about order, not justice; besides, the rebel wasn't Roman.

I will say that I, in some secret way, knew my fate, like someone who has received a revelation in an absurd dream that is quickly forgotten. During the protests, I thought, over and over, about the memory of the people I governed. I also knew of the case of a Greek prisoner who had been sentenced to death, and the scholars remembered him more than Pericles. I learned in that land, now distant, that Eternity depends on that confused and fleeting moment that is life. Rome is not eternal, and one day it will only be a memory of stones and books; and it will not be the best of the Empire that the future will remember.

When everyone demanded that I crucify the rebel and no one knew why, I sought counsel from others less great than I. The Romans didn't care or were amused, so I had to turn, several times, to Joacim of Samaria, a wise man whom I had once sought to understand his people.

"Tell me, Joacim," the governor asked him that day or the day before, "what can I do in these circumstances? I must be a judge, and yet I cannot distinguish clear water from foul. Can I even do anything? I've heard that the rebel himself has foretold his death, just as others of your people foretold his coming."

"The world is in your hands," said the old man.

"No!" shouted the governor, "...it is not yet in my hands. First, I will be Emperor in Rome."

"Perhaps Rome and all the Romes to come will remember you for this day, my king."

"And what will they say of me?" the governor asked, curious.

"How can I know? I am a blind man," replied the old man.

"As blind as anyone. I would give my eyes to see the future!"

"Even if you had a thousand eyes, you would not see it, my king, for the future does not exist for men. It exists only in God, who encompasses all."

"If your God knows it, then the future exists somewhere," reasoned the governor. "If God or the rebel can predict what will happen, then what is to be done has already been done..."

When the rebel stood before me, the governor began to question him, hesitating; he knew it was unworthy of a future Caesar.

"So you are a king?" asked the governor.

"You have said it," said the man, dark and serene as if nothing mattered to him. "I came into this world to bring the Truth. And those who can understand it will listen to me."

"And what is the truth?" the governor hurried to ask, certain he would not receive an answer so grand.

But there was an infinite silence in response. Soon the impatient crowd erupted again: "Release the son of man!" they began to shout, referring to another prisoner who had taken up arms against Rome, not words.

The governor knew that if he chose wrong, Palestine would burn. So many could not be mistaken, so the decision had to be one made in the clear mind of a king.

When the soldiers finished flogging the rebel, the governor brought him out again and said to the people:

"Look, here he is, I have brought him out so you may see that I find no crime in him."

But the people insisted again:

"Crucify him...!"

"Better you take him and crucify him yourselves," said the governor.

"No, we cannot."

Then, the governor saw the Rebel enter and asked him:

"Where are you from, that you put me at this cross-roads?"

But the Rebel did not answer this time, just as he had not answered before.

"Do you not intend to answer me? Do you not know that I have the authority to crucify you or to set you free?"

"You would have no authority if God had not given it to you."

Then I, the governor of Palestine, finally yielded to the crowd or to the arrogance of that Jew.

He handed the rebel over to the stake or to the cross. The rumors and the shouts reached the palace from afar.

They crucified him at noon, and until mid-afternoon, the whole land grew dark. A deep cold covered the palace and perhaps the entire city.

"What is happening, my king?" asked Joacim from some dark corner.

"You cannot see it, but the whole Earth has darkened, and it is because of the Rebel," said the governor.

"Rome and the world will remember you for this day," said the blind man.

"It is not fair!" shouted the governor, "how can I be the guilty one? Do you not say that God knows what has happened and what is to come? If your God knew I would err today, how could I be free not to do so?"

"Listen, my king," said the blind man, "I cannot see the present that you see. Nor can I see the future. Yet now I know, almost as the rebel knew before, that you were wrong. But this knowledge, oh my king, does it erase any of the freedom you had this day to choose?"

Jerusalem, 1995

The Age of Barbarism

In the year of Barbarism the annual journeys to the year thirty-three began. That year was chosen because, according to surveys, the crucifixion of Christ drew the attention of more people in the West, and this social sector was targeted for economic reasons, as the journeys to the past had not been directed, much less funded, by the government of any country, as had once been the case with the first journeys into space, but by a private company. The financial group that made the miracle of time travel possible was Axa, at the behest of the Chief Technologist of Blue Technologies, who suggested infinite profits through the provision of "tourist services," as it was called at the time. Since then, several groups of thirty people have traveled to the year thirty-three to witness the death of the Nazarene, just as ordinary tourists once gathered at the foot of the Chichen Itza pyramid during each equinox to witness the formation of the serpent with the shadows the pyramid cast upon itself.

The main issue Axa encountered was the limited number of tourists who could attend the event at once, which generated profits that did not align with the million-dollar expectations of the investment. Gradually, this number was increased to forty-five, at the risk of drawing the attention of the ancient inhabitants of Jerusalem. Later, the number was kept unchanged at the insistence of one of the company's major shareholders, who argued, reasonably, that preserving this historical event in its original state was the foundation that justified the trips. If each group caused alterations to the events, it would lead to a decline in general interest in undertaking such journeys.

Over time, it became clear that every historical alteration, no matter how minor, was almost impossible to repair. This occurred when one of the travelers failed to respect the rules and attempted to take a souvenir from the site. The most famous case was that of Adam Parcker, who, with incredible skill, managed to cut a triangular piece from the red tunic of the Nazarene, likely at the moment when he collapsed from exhaustion. The theft did not result in any changes to the Holy Scriptures, but it made Parcker rich and famous, as the tiny piece of fabric became worth a fortune. Not a few of the travelers who went to the trouble and expense of traveling back thousands of years did so to see where the Nazarene was missing the "Parcker Triangle."

A few have raised objections to this type of travel, claiming that it will ultimately destroy history without us even noticing. Indeed, it is so: for every change introduced on any given day, infinite changes stem from it, century after century, either fading gradually or multiplying in their effects. To detect even the slightest change in the year thirty-three, it would be futile to consult the Holy Scriptures, as all editions, equally, would bear the mark of the alteration, completely forgetting the original event. There would be a possibility of tracing each change by projecting other trips to years before the Year of Barbarism, but no one would care about such a project, and there would be no way to fund it.

The debate over whether history should remain as it is or whether it is permissible to alter it no longer matters. But the latter is, in any case, dangerous, as it is impossible to foresee the resulting changes that any alteration would produce. We know that any change might not be catastrophic for the human species, but it would be catastrophic for individuals: it would not be us who are alive now, but someone else entirely.

On the opposite side are the most radical religious groups. Barbaria's intelligence services recently discovered that a group of evangelists, belonging to the True Church of God in São Paulo, will make the trip to the year thirty-three. Thanks to the donations of their faithful, the group has managed to raise the multi-million-dollar sum that Axa charges for the ticket. What has not yet been confirmed are the group's intentions. It is said that they plan to blow up Golgotha and set Jerusalem on fire at the moment of the Crucifixion, to bring about the long-awaited End of Times. All of history would disappear; the entire world, including the Jews, would recognize their error, convert to Christianity in the year thirty-three, and the whole world would live under the Kingdom of God, as described in the Gospels. This is disputed by others.

Others cannot understand how travelers can witness the Crucifixion without trying to prevent it. The theological answer is obvious, which is why the least interested in preventing the Messiah's martyrdom are his own followers. But for the rest, who are the majority, Axa has decreed its own ethical rules: "Just as we do not prevent the death of a servant in the claws of a lion when we travel to Africa, we must not prevent the apparent injustices committed against the Nazarene. Our moral duty is to preserve nature and history as they are." The Crucifixion is a heritage of Humanity, but, above all, its rights have been fully acquired by Axa.

Indeed, changes are becoming increasingly inevitable. After six years of trips to the year thirty-three, one can see, at the foot of the cross, soda caps and writings in chemical pencil on the main beam, some of which read: "I have faith in my Lord," while others simply record the name of whoever was there, along with the departure date, so that future generations of travelers will remember them. Of course, the company is also beginning to yield to the pressure of dissatisfied customers, aiming for a radical improvement in services. For example, Barbaria has just sent a technical representative to the year twenty-six to secure the production of five thousand cubic meters of asphalt and negotiate with Pilate the construction of a more comfortable corridor for the Via Dolorosa, which will make the journey less tiring for travelers and, moreover, would be a merciful gesture toward the Nazarene, who more than once injured his feet on the stones he couldn't see in his path. It has been calculated that the improvement will not result in changes to the Holy Scriptures, as they show no particular concern for the city's urban planning.

With these measures, Axa aims to shield itself from the flood of complaints it has been facing due to alleged service deficiencies, having recently had to deal with very costly lawsuits from clients who spent a fortune and did not return satisfied. The reason for the complaints is not always the intense heat of Jerusalem or the congestion that traps the city on the day of the Crucifixion. Above all, it is due to the unmet expectations of the travelers. The company defends itself by saying that the Holy Scriptures were not written under its quality control, but are merely historical documents and, therefore, exaggerated. Where the Nazarene dies, instead of a deep and chilling night, the sky merely darkens due to an excessive concentration of clouds, and nothing more. Catholics have declared that this event, like all those mentioned in the Gospels, should be taken in its symbolic value rather than as a mere description. But most people were not satisfied with Axa's response nor with that of Pope John XXV, who came to the defense of the multinational, thanks to which people can now be closer to God.

Athens, 2005

The Mission

When he learned that he had been chosen to go to war, his heart leapt into his throat.

He would soon turn nineteen. He had prepared his whole life, his short life, for that moment. At one point, he feared that the war would find him too old, but the news and events of the past few months had gradually left him with the certainty that his time had come.

It was not a surprise, but he could not avoid the emotions that brought him to his knees, bent over the ground, crying with joy. He ran his hand over his chest, where years earlier he had tattooed the name of God, and felt that he was alive. The hour, his most glorious hour, had arrived. He knew he might die soon, but he would do so for his people and for his faith.

His mother cried after him, when she was alone in the kitchen, but she was consoled by the pride of a brave son, free from the vain rebellions typical of other young people who did not share their values. She remembered the toys he had loved most, the words he repeated most often as a child, his childhood dreams of flying to the moon in a ball of fire, his impossible questions: "Why does it rain? Why does the sun rise?", and others that were easier: "Where do people go when they die? Why are we born if we have to die?" Nothing in her routine changed. The kitchen, feigning joy, and hiding her true emotions were her mission on earth. To think otherwise was to increase the pain of all that was inevitable.

The young soldier remembered his first spiritual guide revealing to him the passion and the sweetness of eternal truth, which had so often shielded him from madness. On the contrary, he had learned that fear was, at its core, the source of all strength and the deepest path to true faith. Those who do not fear do not believe.

He had learned that death does not exist for those who have lived a fruitful life. Death does not exist for those who have served their nation and fallen as heroes fighting for the values of their ancestors. Hell, oblivion, nothingness were reserved for those who believed in nothing. To some extent and for the same reason, he respected and valued all the enemies who would die on the battlefield. Heaven did not await them, but they would undoubtedly escape the hell reserved for the cynics and the unbelievers. Because even the enemies were necessary to fulfill a destiny, and nothing happened without God's approval.

In combat, he eliminated a hundred enemies. He did not remember any particular face. He had hardly been able to see any of them clearly. But he did remember the taste of fear in his saliva and the smell of blood and dust that one night surrounded him and his comrades, many of whom did not return. He did remember that in the face of the vertigo of fear, it was enough for him to repeat three times the prayers he had learned from his first pastor to regain his courage and rise with a fury that was enough to destroy ten with a single shot.

God gave strength to the warrior and victory to his people. The danger of false idols and barbaric customs had passed, at least until the next trial. For years, the children listened to the hero with infinite admiration. The people honored him until a moderate period of peace arrived, and the hero fell into oblivion and poverty.

However, he knew the world was not a safe place, and soon God's nation would be threatened again, because that was how it had always been, and always, not without blood and pain, the truth had prevailed.

The unusual truce lasted twenty long years. Twenty years of peace and almost twenty of irresponsible joy. Until the skies were once again shaken by terrible explosions and filled with fire.

The old hero marched to war at nearly forty, knowing that this time he would not return. This time he would not receive the fleeting glory of his compatriots, the short-lived fruits of the earth, but the eternal glory of Huitzilopochtli, the most powerful of all gods, the eternal one who had demonstrated for thousands of years that everything else is false and perishable. Everything changes and is destroyed every fifty-two years. Except for Huitzilopochtli and the eternal gods of the eternal Aztec empire.

Gainesville, 2011

Guadalupe de Blanco

Sierra Vista, Arizona. 11:10 PM

On a moonless night, Guadalupe de Blanco crossed the border on her knees. She ate the desert sand and watered the soil of Arizona with the blood from her feet.

On Saturday at 3 PM, she stumbled upon a warm water bottle, the kind that the brother dogs throw into the desert in hopes of saving some dying soul.

On Sunday, she fell asleep very slowly, hoping not to wake up the next day. But she woke up, nearly suffocated on a large stain her body had left on the stone. She recognized the vaginal halo of the Guadalupe who had cradled her all night and returned her to the world with love and without mercy. Immediately, she felt the early rigor of the sun, once again slowly working to suck the water from her skin, her flesh, and her brain, the water she had won from the luck of the previous day. Then she put her still moist and beating heart back into her chest, stood up, and in obedience to the Cosmos, kept walking.

Two days later, a coyote found her. Furious, he muttered that the business wasn't worth it anymore. He muttered and spat tobacco. Guadalupe walked in his company and by the promise that her agony had ended. The coyote complained several times about the merchandise. The land was no good, it was dry, the fire rose from the stones, the jimadores didn't pay.

So far that season, he had taken care of nineteen Mexicans, eight Hondurans, five Salvadorans, two Colombians, and someone from further south, a crazy Chilean or Argentine looking for thrills. Most of them short with broad backs, square heads, and mouths of stone. Few words and much hunger and distrust. He had fed them, and one day, upon returning, he found only an empty house.

The house stood at the foot of a ravine as red as the blood of the quetzal. Inside, it smelled of loneliness and beer. Given its size, it didn't seem to have been the refuge for so many people.

Guadalupe's comment didn't sit well with him. At least it was cool shade.

"Guadalupe," he said, smiling, "why have you come to the States?"

"Necessity brought me, sir."

"Necessity is a serious thing," he said, and with skill, he covered her mouth.

Her eyes swelled with tears and terror. The blonde was young and had lips as soft as honey. Her eyes were dark but clear. How to say it? Her breath was agitated and without wrinkles. Like a breath of pleasure, but she didn't understand it that way. The useless little cries were more soft than irritating. That's why she was saved, because I can't stand it when, in the end, they don't recognize good work. I had gone through so many shapeless women that I wasn't going to deny myself that little angel sent from heaven.

Lupita cried all night, but I couldn't tell what kind of crying it was. Whimpers. She called for her mother and someone named "chiquito," who must have been the child she left on the other side. They're worse than dogs. Dogs don't leave their puppies.

In the end, I got tired of all the melancholy, and the next day I cut off a lock of her hair and let her go back the way she came.

She stumbled over the rocks as if I might change my mind, as if I were incapable of keeping my word. She left sniffling like a little girl. It looked more like a cold. The flu. She grabbed her things and left. Crying, of course, like a Magdalene. And the truth is, I regretted it soon after. That girl needed someone to protect her, and I needed someone like her, a butterfly flirting with the flames of the fire, live and in person, not just lying down every night with her lovely memory. Who knows if I have a son out there and don't know it. Or a daughter.

Who knows if in fifteen years I might run into her, light as a little bird, blonde and pretty just like Lupita was.

Such is the poor life of a coyote.

Newark, 2008.

Margaret

Every Tuesday night Margaret would arrive with her folders of notes and teaching materials. Every Tuesday night, María José and Ernesto listened attentively. Margaret was a government social worker who taught parents how to raise their children. These officials pay a lot of attention to Hispanic families because it's well known that they come from a macho and violent culture. The training consisted of a long forty-minute talk, plus a ten-minute educational video and a ten-minute practical demonstration, which added up to an hour, at the end of which María José and Ernesto signed a paper telling the government that the program was working.

On the 8th, Ernesto came home in a bad mood from the construction site, fifteen minutes before Margaret, and had to make a Herculean effort to stay focused on the week's lesson. If it weren't for the fact that he would be seen as a bad father and worse husband, he would have said to let him lie on the couch for fifteen minutes with a glass of wine. But he resisted. It was his will and also his job to resist, to show the government worker and everyone else that he could come home from work exhausted and sometimes humiliated—Ernesto considered it humiliating to follow any order against his will and in silence—and still change diapers, wash dishes, and sing at the same time.

But in the last ten minutes of that day, Luisito was more restless than usual. He threw the same tantrum three times that kids have at that age, screaming at the top of his lungs followed by rolling on the floor, all over a pencil that his father had denied him as dangerous. Ernesto simply said "no," first and "*no!*" after, which led to the specialist's intervention:

"Try not to say no. That's the word children hear the most. That's why they reproduce negativity in their behavior."

"What can we do in these cases, Margaret?" asked María José.

"Hug him. You should comfort him. Tell him you love him. Show him he won't lose your love over spilled yogurt. That will build his self-esteem and trust in adults."

"See, Ernesto. You always say parents are educators, not comforters."

Before she finished the sentence, Luisito threw the yogurt on the carpet, and Ernesto, in another careless moment, told him not to do it again. But he said it with such vehemence that it surprised Margaret.

As a good professional, without losing her calm and soft, almost sensual tone, Margaret explained that what Ernesto had done was an example of a very common mistake among Latino parents.

"What?" asked Ernesto, almost regretful.

"Raising your voice at the child."

"What was I supposed to do?"

"In these cases, the Association strongly recommends explaining to the child that yogurt doesn't go on the carpet. In fact, to avoid hurting his feelings, you should have approached the child and played with the spilled yogurt. After all, you'll still have to use a stain remover. It's the same work."

"Yes, it sounds very practical, as always. But I don't think it's such a big deal." When you have a boss like mine and a kid like Luisito, then you'll know what it's like to live in a world drawn with thick boundaries.

"Mr. Campos," Margaret reasoned calmly, always avoiding eye contact, "the child is two years old... He'll have plenty of time to learn all that."

"The sooner the better. Besides, I don't think he'd understand an explanation about the inconvenience of throwing yogurt on the carpet every time he's full."

"From your words, I gather your childhood wasn't easy."

"True."

"Did you witness violent scenes in your family home?"

"Yes, a few."

"Did your father hit your mother?"

"No, not at all. If anything, it was the other way around. But not even that. My mother was a calm woman too."

"Then?"

"For example, more than once I had to watch when one of my father's cows died, and he had no choice but to skin it."

"Skin it? What does that mean?"

"Take off its hide. He had to slit its belly open with a knife, like this, from top to bottom, and carefully skin it to at least save the hide."

"How awful! And how old were you?"

"Five or six."

"My God! That's enough to traumatize a child. Didn't your father care? What level of education did he have?"

"My father had finished high school and that was it. And because of that, he couldn't afford to lose the whole cow. At least that way he salvaged the hide, and since we were in the Pampas, even though he told me to go far away, I could still see him skinning the dead animal from a hundred meters away. And I'm not even telling you about when a ranch hand had to kill a pig by stabbing it in the heart. The thing screamed like a pig."

"My God!"

"Someone had to do it. Everyone had to eat. What did you eat today?"

"Salad. What else do you remember?"

"Sometimes the family of the deceased would be around, a pair of pigs that would start mating in front of me. Those things you don't forget."

"How awful! All of that explains the violence."

"Excuse me, what violence?"

"The violence in Latin countries."

"Yet I'm not a criminal. I've never killed anyone, and I detest all kinds of violence. For example, I can't stand that out of the hundred TV channels I have here, at least ninety are always showing someone being killed, having an eye gouged out, or getting shot in the head. Do you want me to show you?"

"That's not necessary. But all of that is fiction."

"Sex can also be acted out, and yet it's taboo or pornography. If you're not careful, kids can see fifteen murders a night. But if two people share a French kiss, it's censored. You can depict a crime, but you can't depict love."

"My pastor always says something very wise. The evil of the world begins when sex is confused with love."

"No, I don't confuse them. But I also don't see them as necessarily incompatible. Or is it not possible that sex and love could be the same thing sometimes? I mean, in such a materialistic world, every now and then they might be the same thing, by miracle or coincidence. Even if only in representation. But no, for public morality, sex is never love and is always obscene. So it must be banned and preached against, to forget that evil wasn't born with sex but with the crime against one's neighbor. But to tell you the truth, the pigs in the Pampas taught me not only that sex is something natural but also explained what my parents didn't know how to explain in a more scientific way. But on TV, when a guy or a beautiful woman—sorry I didn't say 'handsome man'; it's not that I'm sexist, it's that I'm heterosexual—when some Adonis or Amazon aims at the forehead of some poor soul and blows them away with a transcontinental missile-like shot, neither of them says a single bad word. That's prohibited and carefully controlled."

"Not in Latin countries?"

"No. On the TVs in our countries, they swear like sailors."

"Please, Ernesto!" María José complained, noticing that the conversation had completely derailed.

"What? Isn't it true?" Ernesto insisted. "Over there, people kiss more often than they kill, and women walk around half-naked."

"Part of the macho culture."

"Yes, they walk around half-naked like in all countries where machismo reigns. Except for Muslim women, who, due to their cultural backwardness, dress more conservatively." Because machismo doesn't know how to dress women. It either dresses them with too little clothing or too much. Never in the right measure, like in the United States, where women are free.

"You wouldn't deny that machismo prevails in your countries,"

"Many things prevail. Of course, we all have flaws. I'll give you that. We also have problems with street crime, organized crime, the organized poverty of the favelas. But in general, we like death, blood, and the thrill of Agatha Christie-style crime or Arnold Schwarzenegger-style killing machines less. At least when we don't have our own cinema. After all, you have to admit that *The Terminator* had very good special effects. A whole science."

"I repeat, all of that is fiction. Our children's education programs have been in place for years, and in all the models we've implemented, violence is prohibited, whether it's saying 'no,' as you've done, or scolding a child for spilling yogurt on the carpet. Children replicate what they see."

"Yet in this house, no one spills yogurt on the carpet, and we don't have the habit of sticking fingers into electrical outlets. To me, it's in the child's nature, and since in nature there are no electrical outlets or carpets to care for, there's no choice but to educate. And a clear *no* is better than a *maybe* with complexes."

"I hope you're not trying to give us lessons. Studies clearly indicate that we must eradicate all forms of violence in a child's education."

"I'm glad. I already told you I don't condone any form of violence. The problem is defining it. It's also violence to make a child believe the world is as soft as a panda bear."

"For years, we've categorized and eradicated every type of violence, and I can tell you that all these plans have been a success."

"How do you deduce that they've been a success?"

For brief moments, Margaret seemed annoyed by Ernesto's questioning. Without rushing, she began organizing her papers in the blue folder.

"Many studies conclusively demonstrate it," she replied.

"Since when do those experiments date?"

"From the sixties and seventies."

"Let's see, let me think. If my numbers don't fail me, all the soldiers, generals, politicians, and pastors who participated in and supported the last war in Iraq, to name just one of many, were educated as children under those non-violence methods. How is it that children so shielded from strong words, parental discipline, death, and sex in all its forms are capable of bombing markets and cities full of children? Children like mine, like yours. Do you know how many people have died in Iraq? Over half a million, if we consider Iraqis to be people, of course."

"It's different."

"Yes, it's different. Everything is done with the purest language, with perfect grammar. Freedom, democracy, God, civilization. The blood doesn't splatter. The dead don't have grieving relatives. Those young men—with high self-esteem, no doubt—those young men who go to kill fanatics in other countries think they're in a *video game*. They press a button and don't even have to witness the unpleasant spectacle of what they're doing. And if one of them sees something live and in person, that is, some dismembered body outside the blue and green screen, they send them to prestigious psychologists, programs that have been successful, theories scientifically proven and endorsed by studies from renowned doctors. And those who don't go to war or commit suicide upon returning turn to abusing Coca-Cola, in the best case, or cocaine, in the worst. Did you know that this country, with children so well-educated and shielded from sex and the violence of saying *no*, is the world's largest consumer of narcotics? Did you know that in the country where bad words and the occasional beautiful backside on television are prohibited, where a look can be considered sexual harassment—in fact, here no woman can withstand being looked in the eye; when you look at them, they avert their gaze as if they were nuns being courted—nevertheless, and perhaps because of that, it's full of sexual psychopaths and serial killers? In our backward countries, killers murder because they're beasts. They shoot someone. Serial killing is almost unheard of, because it's an invention of the systematic production and reproduction of things. The killers in those backward countries don't calculate, don't press buttons, and don't eliminate two hundred thousand people in a single day. That's only possible in a country where children are raised under the best psychological theories of non-violence and modesty."

Margaret didn't lose her composure. She held it in so it wouldn't slip away. She glanced at her watch. With great elegance, she said it had gotten late. Three minutes late. The parents signed. Margaret confirmed the number of words Luisito could pronounce. 33. Normal for his age, but if by the next visit he hadn't been able to pair a noun with an adjective, he'd have to be referred to a specialist. She gathered her things gently and said goodbye with her usual smile.

But a second after the door closed, she was heard saying:

"Fuck you."

Ernesto couldn't tell if the tone was one of contained rage or the same unflappable tone as always. What he was sure of was that Margaret had wanted to be heard. The best opportunity of her life to say a bad word in public.

Newark, 2008

Tales of a Novelist

The Walled Society

Over the years, and thanks to careful observation of his patients, Dr. Salvador Uriburu had discovered that most of the population of Calataid lacked the European origin they boasted about. In their eyes, in their hands, lingered the *black* slaves who repaired the walls in the 9th century and surely the older slaves who built the cisterns in the time of Garama. In their ritual gestures lingered the followers of Kahina, the desert priestess of Africa who converted to Judaism before the arrival of Islam. Within the white minority, diversity was also notable, but it had been put on hold while they were busy considering themselves the representative (and founding) class of the town. The same blue eyes could be found behind Russian eyelids or behind Irish ones; the same blond hair could cover a Germanic skull or a Galician one. How was it possible—Salvador Uriburu had written—that such a diverse people could be so racist and, at the same time, overflow with so much patriotism, so much fanatical love for the same flag? How can one venerate the whole while despising the parts that make it up? Unless patriotic veneration is nothing more than the Necessary Lie that one part feeds to the others to use them for its own benefit.

In one of his last public appearances, in May 1967, in the hall of notables at the Libertad Club, Dr. Uriburu had conducted an exercise that annoyed the new traditionalists, once they were able to decipher the critique. Salvador Uriburu had drawn, on a blackboard, a series of at least 15 triangles, circles, and squares. When he asked those present how many types of drawings they saw there, everyone agreed they saw three. When he asked them to choose one of those three types, they all chose the group of triangles, and the doctor asked again how many groups they saw within the triangles. Everyone said there were at least two groups: a group of isosceles triangles and a group of right-angled triangles.

"More or less isosceles and more or less right-angled," said one with insight, noting that the drawings weren't perfect.

"The figures aren't perfect," confirmed Salvador Uriburu, "just like humans. And like humans, everyone first saw the differences, what the figures had that was different, before seeing what they had in common."

"That's not true," someone said, "the triangles have something in common. Each one has three sides, three angles."

"The circles and squares also have something in common: they're all geometric figures. But no one observed that there was also a single group of drawings, the group of geometric figures."

Salvador Uriburu didn't name names or clarify the example, as was his habit. Let the shoe fit whoever it fits. But after months of discussing the doctor's strange and pedantic presentation of the little figures, Pastor George Ruth Guerrero concluded that this kind of thinking came to the good doctor from the sect of humanists and, surely, from the Illuminati.

"The group of geometric figures," concluded the pastor, with his index finger raised, "represented humanity, and each group of figures represented a race, a religion, a deviation, and so on. The humanists want to make us believe that truth doesn't exist; that the faith of the Moors and the Jews is the same as the true faith of Christians, the race of the chosen and the race of sinners, the morals of our fathers and the sodomy of the moderns, the dresses of our women and the shameless nudity of Nigerian women."

They accused him of being a Gnostic. It was known, through rumors and magazines from France, that the Heterodox had conquered the rest of Europe with an unusual belief: truth did not exist; any heresy could be taken as a substitute for true faith and logical reason. And it was said that someone was trying to introduce all of this into Calataid.

The allusion was direct, but Dr. Uriburu did not respond. The last time he entered the hall of notables, in August 1967, it was expected that he would declare whether he was for or against this superstition, that he would finally define which side he was on. Instead, he came out with another of his figures that did not align with his profession as a scientist, much less with that of a believer, which demonstrated his irreversible descent into mysticism, into the sect of the Illuminati who, it was said, gathered every Thursday in an unknown chamber of the ancient cisterns.

"Once, a man climbed a sand dune," he said, "and upon reaching the summit, he decided that this was the only dune in the desert. However, he soon noticed that others had done the same, from other summits. Then he said that his, the one beneath his feet, was the true one. Another man, perhaps a woman, decided to descend from her dune and climbed another, and then another, until she understood (perhaps on the highest dune) that the dunes were many, infinite for her strength. Then, tired, she said that the desert was not a particular dune of sand, but all the dunes together. She said that there were some dunes taller and others smaller, that a single handful of sand, from any of them, did not represent a particular dune but the entire desert, but that none, like none of the dunes, was the desert, completely. She also said that the dunes moved, that the true dune, which allowed the only perspective of the desert and of itself, constantly changed in size and location, and that ignoring this was an inseparable part of any singular truth. Unlike another exhausted traveler, this discovery did not lead him to deny the existence of all the dunes, but the arbitrary pretense that there was only one in the vastness of the desert. He denied that a handful of sand had less value and less permanence than that arbitrary and pretentious dune. That is, he denied some ideas and affirmed others; he was not indifferent to the eternal search for truth. And for this, he was equally persecuted in the name of the desert, until a sandstorm put an end to the dispute."

An indescribable silence followed the doctor's new enigma. Then a suppressed murmur filled the hall. Someone took the floor to announce the end of the meeting and reminded everyone of the date of the next one. The bell rang; everyone stood up and left without greeting him. He knew that it also bothered them that he doubted the tolerance and freedom of Calataid, resorting to metaphors as if he were a victim of the Inquisition or living in the times of the barbaric Nero.

Uriburu remained seated, looking out the window at the old and rapacious men passing by on bicycles who could not see him, with his hands in the pockets of his coat, playing with a handful of sand. He lost his mind twenty days later. A strange diagnosis, in his own handwriting, concluded that Calataid suffered from "social autism." Autism, his books said, is the product of the accelerated growth of the brain which, instead of increasing intelligence, reduces it or renders it useless due to the pressure of the brain mass against the walls of the skull. For Dr. Uriburu, more concerned with archaeology than biology, the walls of Calataid had caused the same effect with the growth of its pride or population. Therefore, it was useless to try to cure the *individuals* if society was sick. In fact, assuming that society and individuals are two different things is an artifice of sight and medicine, which identifies bodies, not spirits. And Calataid was incapable of relating two different facts with a common explanation. More so: it was incapable of recognizing its own memory, scandalously engraved in the stones, in the damp voids of its entrails, and denied or concealed by the most recent invention of a tradition.

Athens, 2005

Journalism

He wrote a brief article justifying the events of the week that was beginning to fade into the past and sent it to the editor of *La Santa Alfaguara*. Years earlier, when he entered the town hall, he had begun by collaborating in the layout and writing of *La Aldaba*, until the mayor shut it down in 1977, to create *La Alfaguara* of Calataid, inspired by the fountain in the central courtyard of the town hall and in line with the more spiritual profile he intended to give the new newspaper. *La Aldaba*, founded by his own father in 1952, during the time of the Medinas, was published once a week, without color and almost without photos. With the death of the doctor and the resignation of some of its frequent contributors, *La Aldaba* began to change its style and, at times, increased its readership. The printed typeface greatly impressed people who were only familiar with the handwritten notes of their neighbors, often scribbled in a store notebook. Around that time, Basílides managed to convince the previous editor of *La Aldaba*, a nearly blind and deaf old man, to include a page of astrological predictions, like those still seen in the fashion magazines that arrived before 1962. And who better than himself for this task, as he had a telescope at home and knew a bit about astronomical calculations? No one ever questioned where these predictions came from, and the editor soon forgot that the author was the new treasury employee. Although, after all, his method was reasonable, or at least consistent with the theory of the four elements: if it is true that those born under the same sign inherit the same psychological traits and even the same fate from the stars, then it is enough to study one person per sign to understand the rest of humanity and what possibilities each has in the near future. For example, Basílides knew that the nanny was a Virgo. So, when he saw her depressed or anxious, he would write for that week: "Virgo, watch your anxiety." And then he would add a specific event: "you will receive good news in your work life," because he knew that in a certain month her mother would give her a raise. He also knew that Don Ferrando's wife was a Scorpio, and when he saw her being a bit more provocative than usual, he would write for Scorpio: "In love, a need for change…" Of course, he never believed in astrology, but at least he was honest, albeit a skeptical one: if all the men and women of Virgo were not depressed that week and not receiving a raise, if all the men and women of Scorpio did not have the same bad luck in love, then the horoscope was not useful for what it claimed to be. And it wasn't his fault. Moreover, he never fell into the habit of recommending a different lottery number for each sign, nor into the custom of associating one sign with artistic skills and another with scientific skills, as he had already noticed in encyclopedias that the births of artists and scientists were scattered indifferently throughout the year. The truth is that since then, almost a hundred more copies were sold, and no one was ever dissatisfied with the predictions of *La Aldaba*, even when they read a sign that wasn't theirs or when Basílides got the order wrong. In passing, he added essential *fragments* of Heidegger that he took from his father's cupboard, which frightened the nanny and deprived him of greetings from his coworkers.

"*At the beginning of its history, absolute knowledge must be other than at the end. Certainly, but this otherness does not mean that at the beginning [there was light and] knowledge* was in no way yet *absolute knowledge. On the contrary, precisely at the beginning it is already absolute knowledge, but absolute knowledge that has not yet arrived at itself, that has not yet* become *other [or the same] but is only the other. The other: it, the absolute, is other, that is, it is* not absolute, *it is relative. The non-absolute is not yet absolute. But this not-yet is the not-yet* of the absolute, *that is, the non-absolute is not in some way and despite it but precisely because it is absolute, because it is [the] non-absolute: this not, by reason of which the absolute can be relative, belongs to the absolute itself, it is* not different *from it, that is, it does not* lie beside it, *extinguished and dead. The word 'not' in 'non-absolute' in no way expresses something that, being present for itself, lies* beside *the absolute, but the not alludes to a mode of the absolute.*

"(*Martin Heidegger:* Phenomenology of Spirit. *Winter semester course, Freiburg, 1930-31. Edition by Der Mann ohne*

Eigenschaften, 1953. Translation, introduction, and notes: Heidi und seine brüder, Heide und Heger.)"

Athens, 2004

Public Works

Just five years ago, Basílides dared to invent mockeries and absurdities like these in *La Aldaba*, until the order came to shut down the weekly for a year. This prevented the revelation of a discovery made by the pseudo-astrologer himself in the archives of the Department of Public Works at the city hall, which would have, at the very least, crowned the series with a flourish. Dated August 1945, the project for a "promenade" that had been partially constructed and then buried by the sands and the memory of Calataid had been forgotten. The old plans, patiently drawn and copied in blue ink, along with the lengthy descriptive reports, still revealed a sudden progressive enthusiasm that gradually faded. "Perhaps the project's failure was due to the lack of originality among the Santistas, to a sudden desire to copy the successes of others that arrived through American films and European magazines," Basílides had written in the article that never saw publication.

The story of the project began one day when the mayor, Don Juan Medina Medina (1859-1963), decided to invigorate the city's activity with a grand public work that would immortalize his name. The idea that faced the least resistance (and ultimately won enthusiastic applause in the end) was to build a promenade that would run along the outer limits of the city. Only one detail remained to be resolved: How to build a promenade without first having a sea, or at least a river? The solution, according to the municipal engineer, Don Daniel Medina (1864-1963), was to take advantage of the contour lines to identify a possible channel to fill with water. At the Assembly of Aldermen, he explained, with incomplete details, everything he had learned at the University of Granada about contour line calculations, which did little to clarify the feasibility of the project but instead doubled the public's enthusiasm. The contour lines appeared, because there is always a point lower than another, but there was no way to make even the smallest stream pass through there. None of this made the authorities change their minds, and so they ended up building their longed-for Promenade. To fill the bed of the new river, part of the ancient northern wall was demolished, and the sewers were diverted toward it, which seemed like a perfect idea: not only would a promenade be created for the people within the walls, but it would also solve some sanitation issues that had plagued the citizens for many years. It was said, for example—and later, Dr. Salvador Uriburu shared the same opinion—that almost all the cisterns, wells, and the large communal water tank were contaminated by the fecal waste the city produced daily. But this claim, especially after the failure of the project, was considered an insult to Calataid, and no one dared to reconsider it. According to Daniel Medina's plan, trees and flowers would be planted on either side of the future Sewer-Promenade to mask the odor produced by the exposed wastewater, which was often accompanied by human waste in its initial state, making it far less attractive than had been imagined during the voting process. But the townspeople showed their goodwill toward Progress and chose not to raise objections to such an important project initiated by the authorities, bringing them, even if only on a small scale, closer to the aquatic wonders of the Seine in Paris or the Thames in London. Still, this had been a local stroke of genius, which already had its merit, according to Basílides. But as quickly as its construction, its abandonment and oblivion were organized during the unforgettable sixties. After Algeria's independence in 1962 and the horrors of the civil war, it became clear that the demolition of thirty-three percent of the San Fernando wall, used for the new construction, had been the worst sin committed in Calataid in its long existence. The wall remained with this wound, a reminder of the barbarity of progress, until everyone forgot the cause that had provoked it, and its reconstruction began in 1963. Since it was impossible to locate the original stones, it was decided to deconstruct two towers to repair the historical damage caused by the Medinas. The two tallest towers were chosen where, for some time and thanks to the new immigrants, refugees of the war, two radio antennas had been installed, earning one of them the nickname "the Tower of Babel." The ears of

Calataid were removed in a single day, which was met with relief and celebration by most of the population.

Athens, 2004

The Boss

WHEN HE WAS NERVOUS, the mayor would count the fingers on his hand. But on Friday night, as he tried to read some magazines saved from the fire at the Matriz, he noticed something strange: he had nine. He counted again: nine, once more. Then, he repeated this operation until, overwhelmed by the evidence, he looked up at a Goya painting and began to think. He had always believed he had ten fingers. Where could this conviction have come from? He had seen it in other people. The engineer had ten, though he wasn't entirely sure, because he had never counted them. But the engineer always talked about the decimal system, or something like that. The engineer was good at counting and had told him that everything repeats in tens because we have ten fingers. But do we all have ten fingers?—the mayor wondered, now somewhat nervous. He had nine, and no one had ever told him. Maybe they had hidden it from him, because people were always afraid of upsetting him. "Deep down, they're scared of me," he said to himself and smiled proudly. However, no one had told him he had nine fingers when he was just a bartender at the Libertad club either. Maybe people were already afraid of him back then. Or maybe he had lost a finger after being elected mayor. All those people around him, touching him, wanting to take a piece of him as a memento. But when, exactly, could he have lost a finger? That hurts a lot, or it must hurt, so it's unlikely to go unnoticed, neither by the one who loses it nor by the people around him. Or the pain had been so intense that it had caused amnesia, like when one sees something they don't want to see and faints or wakes up from the nightmare. Or was he losing fingers on his hand the way diabetics lose toes, without pain? What had become of the lost finger? Which of the bumps on his hands had once been the root of the missing finger? He looked around. He looked at the painting: a woman holding the coffin with the sardine was smiling, showing five fingers on one hand. The other hand wasn't visible, but it was safe to assume it also had five fingers, since animal nature tends to be symmetrical, if not in its proportions, at least in the number of elements that compose it. Although the heart was only one and not in the middle, like the nose or the penis. It was off-center, slightly tilted, perhaps proof of its imperfection and the chaos of all the feelings that flowed through its valves: love, hate, joy, sorrow... A true mess. But aside from this detail, the rest of nature is symmetrical: men, women, trains, and tree leaves. As soon as he finished this reasoning, he felt happy: he really did seem very intelligent. There was a reason they had elected him governor of the entire city, that is, of every known human being in the vicinity. If it weren't for the desert that surrounds them, he would also be governor of the neighboring villages. He would have an empire. Even the deputy mayor, who always took care of everything and who had pushed him into politics, said the same thing. He had become mayor because of his prodigious intelligence and his oratory skills. The deputy mayor always told him that.

One, two, three... nine. He took off his shoes and counted again: this time he reached ten, not with relief but with a hint of concern, because the number confirmed that he was missing a finger on one of his hands. He went back to his hands and counted backward, trying to determine which hand was missing the finger in question. Nine, eight, seven... one. They were all there. No, he had done it wrong. He should start at ten, and if he reached two, it was because he was truly missing a finger and, in the process, he would know which hand it belonged to. He counted again and discovered he was missing one on his left hand. Though all of this was debatable, like deciding when the new millennium would begin, whether in the year 2000 or 2001. It all depends on whether we consider the existence of a year zero, which doesn't exist, just as there is no zero finger, but we start with one... What if he really was missing a finger? Of course, he hadn't noticed it before because he always signed with his right thumb. He looked at both hands at the farthest distance his arms would allow and compared one to the other: he was missing the left index finger, which demonstrated the limitations of mathematical logic. Where it was missing, there was a kind of bump. The hand looked more like a kind of swan. He knew from the photos in the books in the commune's basement. He felt annoyed: if he had discovered an extra finger, it would have been different. Maybe he would have felt proud. But a missing finger unsettled him, and he didn't know why. For a moment, the idea crossed his mind to force his officials to have no more than nine fingers, combined on both hands, but he dismissed it immediately, telling himself quietly that he was a democratic and tolerant ruler. Ordering fingers to be cut off without justification was a savage practice of the camel herders who spoke gibberish. Of course, he could find a reason. There's always a reason for everything. Tax evaders, for example, deserved a fair and exemplary punishment. All it would take was a decree that the assembly would heatedly debate for two or three months before finally confirming such a necessary measure. It's better to lose a finger than a hand, a tooth than a head. That way, half the population would be missing a finger... But it would be the less proud half, and he would belong to that ungrateful group of the damned. Therefore, it was better to proceed the other way around. He could at least promote in rank all those who were missing a finger. Yes, that. That would be something positive, because it would teach others that what matters in life is personal growth despite some deficiency. And soon that deficiency would turn into a virtue, a mark of distinction. Yes, he knew it—as always, one tries to distinguish oneself from the poor, the underprivileged, but they always end up imitating the customs of the nobility. Surely, in a few years everyone would end up cutting off a finger. Damn it, he said, slamming the table with his five-fingered hand.

He wanted to think of something else. From under a pile of old papers, he picked up a *La Aldaba* from 1974. On the back page, the madman with the horn had written a long quote from Martin Heidegger. He read it with the usual skepticism in such cases: Phenomenology of Spirit by Hegel. It was in German. Or in an old Spanish, hence its difficulty, with those horrible *lo, las, les, los* that only served to confuse.

"If only at the end absolute knowledge is itself in a total form, knowledge that knows, and if it is this in the becoming *as such, insofar as* it arrives *at itself, but only arrives at itself insofar as knowledge becomes other, then at the beginning of its journey toward itself* it is not yet *with and within itself. It must still be other and, moreover, even without yet having* become *other. Absolute knowledge must be other at the beginning of the experience that consciousness has with itself, an experience that, moreover, is nothing other than the movement, the history in which the* coming-to-itself in the becoming-other» occurs.

He cleaned his glasses and took a pencil to correct the grammatical errors:

«*Thus, if in its phenomenology knowledge must make with itself the experience in which it experiences what it is not and what* [E] *precisely in that is with it, then this can only be so if the knowledge itself that makes (fulfills) the experience, in some way, is already absolute knowledge. Martín Heidegger...»*

He looked at the finger that wasn't there. He couldn't forget it so easily, like someone who wakes from a nightmare and realizes it's real. He decided to close *La Aldaba* four or five years ago due to those excessive grammatical errors, following a vote by the Assembly. Then, he reviewed the education programs to recover the lost values, the original spirit of Calataid, the moral reserve of the world in the dark times to come, long foretold by Dr. Uriburu, who shot himself in the mouth to silence his own voice. I eliminated false reproductive education, the blasphemous theory of evolution and all other theories, and replaced them with the teaching of *facts*. «Facts and not theories» was the motto of that campaign, inspired by our pastor George Ruth Guerrero. And although the Assembly resisted, as always, they eventually understood the wise measure, and even the most progressive preferred to lose an eye rather than go blind. But so much effort was not enough, and now the city pays the consequences for its lack of faith.

A woman who was crying or laughing pulled him out of his musings. It was a brief, stifled sob coming from the other side of the corridor door; a moan that repeated like a suppressed echo. He opened the door and fell silent, but he heard nothing more. He closed the door again, leaving a discreet sigh on the other side.

Through the window, he saw several columns of black smoke hastening the sunset. The neighbors had decided to burn mattresses and any items used for rest or pleasure. The collective burning caused some larger fires that destroyed a few houses in Santiago and a few more in San Patricio. In this way, the first prophecy of Aquines Moria was fulfilled.

Athens, 2004

The assistant

The mechanic's assistant was another, though no one ever mentioned him in their speculations. The constable spoke to him two or three times, without making any comment. He was a large man and walked slowly, somewhat hunched over with his head forward, as if trying to hide his enormous height. He had straight blond hair that fell over his eyes, like a beautiful golden helmet covering a lost gaze, probably the only gaze he had, the same one he had kept one day when he woke up without fully waking and which showed how little he understood of the world around him, like someone in the midst of a heavy dream who never quite understands why sunflowers have eyes and farmers have blind seeds on their faces. The legitimate son of the Pessoa family, owners of the taxi cabs and wool workshops on Empedrada Street, he was a rich child and a poor adult, though he never appreciated the difference, which made him a kind of wise idiot. Like all illegitimate or abandoned adopted children, the Pessoa boy thought with half his brain. His father, Don Vero, had traded him for a playmate, for a street urchin called El Trueque, who, when he played with him, always ended up with his food or convinced him to swap the clothes they were wearing.

The shopkeeper had seen potential in the other boy and called him to his side. Eventually, he put him in charge of the business to perpetuate his name and his legacy. Soon after, El Trueque Pessoa exceeded the old man's expectations. Like any successful businessman, he didn't disdain politics and invested as much money in municipal elections as in the purchase of red inks from Mali, which silently replaced the old indigo blue from Libya. He received almost no votes, but this detail didn't prevent him from obtaining a position of trust in the administration and the friendship of Don Josef María de Rodrigo, which, like everything else, was also part of his calculations.

After the death of his mother, Doña Carmen Pessoa, and the sudden senile dementia of Don Vero, Eugenio lost everything without realizing it; which was, in a way, a relief from the injustice. Without resentment, he continued smiling at flies and collecting beetles, because he was terrified of being alone. When this moment came—because it's inevitable, like death, the bird said—he felt uncomfortable with himself and moved his head forward, like someone listening to dance music without dancing. He always had one or two beetles in one of his hands. When no one was looking, he would open his fists and the beetles would climb from the lowest finger to the highest, like armored mountaineers who didn't realize they were climbing from the first finger to the second and from the second to the first, never tiring, until someone passed by and shouted *idiot*. Then the god of cycles would close his fists and hide the insects, frightened, as if he knew that spinning beetles was something dirty, indecent. Because there was also a rumor—only among the men of the town—that the idiot manipulated beetles on the advice or insistence of the priest, who in this way sought to prevent him from masturbating on the side of the roads, where women and even innocent maidens might pass. And since the idiot had been very well endowed by nature, he might give in to the temptation to commit some disgrace. Either his own temptation or that of one of the innocent maidens who often went out at dusk to stroll through the squares and the paths leading into the town, dreaming of the sudden arrival of a soap opera actor. There were debates about the results: it was likely that the priest had succeeded, but in any case, only partially, because if it was always difficult for an intelligent man to control his own nature, it was probably even harder for the idiot. So spinning and crushing beetles only to get new ones could only mean—at least for a doctor from the last century—giving in to temptation, breaking the small, black taboos, and then protecting others as a sign of repentance. But what would happen when there were no more beetles left in the area?

Eugenio Pessoa could well have been my brother. Everyone threw a stone at him when they could, like hens pecking without reason at chicks that limp or suffer from some visible deformity. But I never paid attention, they're

157

very funny, if I get angry I crush them, like Romerito who tried to fly from my hand and I caught him in the air and he couldn't move anymore. Romerito had a red back and little black dots on that red and spoke Spanish, he said yes, yes, he was bad, but those funny ones who throw stones and run away, no, they're not good, says the little priest. To make matters worse, no one ever knew where he got the beetles from, a search that would have puzzled even the brightest minds in the village; and no one ever knew, for certain, what he did with them after he made them dizzy, which always made some people uneasy, because while the first question was mysterious, the second was at least suspicious. I liked the yellow ones, with little red dots. It was said that he killed them, squeezing them in his fists until the cavity of his enormous hands was nullified by the supernatural pressure of his idiocy, which undoubtedly justified the stones the children threw at him. And at night he hunted fireflies in the cemetery, the little green light, the yellow one, the red one I didn't like, but I caught them one by one until there were no more and everything turned dark. The last little yellow light always costs me the most, because it has more space and flies faster than I do. And since it's all dark, I trip and tumble to the ground. He was even known to have drowned some cats, as hard as it is to drown cats in water. There was never any proof of this, not even the absence of a known cat thief , but everyone said the same thing, and it's possible he took pride in those lies. The idiot must have sensed that people respected him—as much as they could respect him—for the same reason they threw stones at him. People respected the mechanic when he broke the donkey's ribs, so why would they bother with someone who enjoyed dizzying beetles? Or was it that people were bothered by the idiot doing something of his own volition? Or did he simply bother them like a lame chicken among healthy ones? Who knows. But it must also be said that he had defenders; of course, there's never a shortage of bad defenders. Some even claimed that the idiot was rather innocent, harmless most of the time, though no one could guarantee anything when he erupted in rage, and that's why they had put him with the mechanic to expend his energy dragging scrap metal from one place to another for no reason. Better a tired idiot than a hundred imagining things. On the other hand, the mechanic needed an assistant who wasn't as smart as he was, since he was a married man; and the one he got couldn't charge much, since he was an idiot.

As for the donkey, I'll say that under my management it fared much worse. As if it were responsible for the Basilisk's complaints, they left it tied to the lamppost, day and night, with a bucket of water ten centimeters outside the circle described by the rope. For two nights in a row, I had to sneak through the scrap metal to bring it water, but the donkey wouldn't budge from its position of sad statue. It stayed there, staring, resting on its crooked legs, as if instead of legs it were propped up on four crutches, with its enormous drooping ears and white eye sockets, its belly sagging more from spinal weakness than from overfeeding, stubbornly refusing to try the water that the kind intruder offered, as if it no longer had any reason to trust any human being and preferred to keep suffering from thirst rather than die poisoned.

On the last night, Ramabad left the bucket against the post, at the risk of being discovered, and the next day he forgot about it. Later, he learned from the amused comment of the greengrocer that the mechanic had put the donkey on a work penance, since, as everyone knows, these small beasts are very stubborn and grumpy, and often refuse to obey. Along with the village idiot, they made it work double shifts, hauling back and forth the carcasses of wheel-less carriages, sometimes bleeding from its sides, where the axles and rusted sheets would dig in when the small beast couldn't move forward and, after the tug, the rope would yank it back with even greater violence. The donkey divided the village in two: the few who frowned upon the mistreatment it endured day after day, and the many who laughed at its crooked legs, twisted from the effort, and died laughing at the brays it let out from time to time when the General of the Golden Helmet raised his stick like a sword. Particularly successful was the anonymous idea of placing an old fine Scottish cloth hat on the donkey, with two holes for its enormous ears to stick out, which the mechanic removed as soon as he saw it from afar, furious because what was pulling the chassis was a donkey, not a man. And since the mechanic wasn't willing to waste his time looking for the culprit of such a mockery, he unleashed all his rage on the already battered ribs of the animal, which had to endure kick after kick for lending its image to such an offense against the human species.

"Don't hit him, boss," said the General. "Look how it cries.

To which the boss responded, shouting: Don't be an idiot, don't you know donkeys always act like this? Every animal has its noise, and that doesn't mean it's crying. Hyenas go ha-ha when they fight, and that doesn't mean they're laughing at something. You'll see that if I hit it with this every time it brays, it'll lose the habit.

Why can a person hate an innocent animal so much? It's impossible to know for sure. The children of Calataid also had a fondness for torturing and killing cats, almost always drowning them in what apparently terrified them the most: water. Still, the cats resisted the sacrifice and would often sink their claws and teeth into the hands of their torturers, giving the latter even more and better arguments. But with the donkey, it wasn't like that. That small beast was incapable of kicking back at anyone. Its sad face and its peaceful nature inspired both pity and anger at the same time, because one couldn't understand how it was able to endure day after day, blow after blow, without taking any action, like any normal human being would.

Over time, the idea took hold that the donkey had birth defects and, probably, was of a flawed breed. Many believed that Lucifer rode on its back from dusk till dawn. Only that could explain a super-animal intelligence that couldn't be its own but was instead borrowed. It was compared to other animals, and it was noted that, unlike every dog, every horse, and even every cat, it was the only one that resisted obeying the mechanic. Therefore, it wasn't wrong for him to want to assert himself, just as a homeowner asserts himself over the ferocity of his dog, the recklessness of his horse, the rebellion of his cats, or the whims of his wife. Of course, "asserting oneself" didn't mean beating it all day long, but quite the opposite: a man who has to resort to violence to earn respect is, in some way, being resisted. Violence could only be a temporary solution. However, the temporary seemed at some point to have no end, and this began to worry the town, which started to suspect that the donkey was incapable of understanding the message and, little by little, the laughter turned to irritation. More than one hothead announced in a circle of friends that, the next time he heard the donkey bray, he himself would go with a stick and break its ribs. Maybe then it would listen to someone else, since it wouldn't listen to its own owner. But even if the donkey was a servant of Lucifer, killing it would have meant offering it as a sacrifice. What was needed was to exorcise the demon with blows.

After the death of Don Luzardo, the donkey spent entire days moving tons of scrap metal, pulling and enduring the mechanic's lashes, without braying in the end. Until one midday, during siesta, it was seen with a rope around its neck, dragging a piece of a carriage down the path of the madwomen. More than one person got up from their siesta, intrigued by the mysterious noise the carcass made on the cobblestones, and saw the donkey walking, slowly and relentlessly.

"It finally learned to pull the scrap metal without braying. But look how much trouble it took, the stubborn bastard!

At first, some laughed and went back to their homes to comment on what they had seen: that donkey was like a person, they said years later. Over time, not only were its antics remembered, but it was also attributed human actions, almost all of them comical, because few things amuse a person more than the human behavior of an animal, just as the opposite frightens and disgusts. The mechanic's donkey preferred chocolate bonbons to cookies, some said; the mechanic's donkey scratched one ear with the hoof of its right hand; the donkey cried when it was yelled at; no, it didn't really cry, it protested like your grandfather; did you ever see the donkey hiding behind a tree to urinate? But while it was alive, it even enraged Father D'Angelo when the General showed up at the church door riding it.

"Can you tell me where you're going, you fool?" was the priest's question, as he intercepted him before the idiot could enter the house of God with the beast and all.

"Me, Father?"

"Who else do you think I'm talking to?"

"Yes, it's true," said the General, showing his beautiful teeth and nodding as if he were confirming something all the while.

"So?"

"So what, Father?"

"I'll repeat the question, more slowly, to see if you can answer: what are you doing on that donkey, with both hooves on the steps of my church?"

"I don't know, Father."

"How is it possible that you do things without knowing! When one doesn't know what they're doing, they stay still, do you understand, boy?"

"Like when I think about the boss's wife and I touch myself down here, Father, and I don't know why I do that, yes."

"Alright, alright, alright, that's enough. I've already told you that stays between us. You don't have to repeat it! That's not a good thing; how many times do I have to tell you? Memorize what I say and don't repeat it. Do you want the whole town to find out what you do? Do you know what they'll say?"

"I don't know, Father."

"They'll say that every day you resemble the donkey more and more!"

"Yes, it's true... That always happens, Father. I'm the most forgetful..."

"Please, boy, get out of here, but first take that crown of thorns off your head before more people see you."

"Yes, Father. I'm the most absentminded. That's it, absentminded. I got on the donkey to take a little ride, and it brought me here all by itself. If you hadn't stopped it, Father, it would've taken me into the temple with it and all."

From this anecdote, which soon became known throughout the town, many conclusions were drawn. About the donkey, the Turk from the shop at the Station said it belonged to the same family line as the one that carried Jesus into Jerusalem, and the next day he made an offer to the mechanic to take the little beast off his hands. But it was considered sacrilegious, and the deal didn't go through. It wasn't a far-fetched assumption—repeated the old man with the big nose, a Christian emigrant from somewhere in Egypt, but a known lover of fantastical stories—since the first donkey had been brought by Berber merchants, meaning it surely came from the Middle East. However, none of these conclusions helped improve the fate of the mechanic's donkey. On the other hand, the anecdote was entirely inconvenient: linking the donkey trying to enter the church with the fool on its back to the donkey that carried Jesus into Jerusalem was dangerously close to equating the Master with the mechanic's assistant, which from every point of view was offensive to the sensibilities of Calataid. And who was to blame for this shameful anecdote?: the donkey, since it wasn't the fool, who didn't know what he was doing, said the bird.

Other stories about the donkey were better adorned with human attributes, which he surely didn't know about or despised. The truth is that, the time he was seen going up the path of the madwomen, he was alone and with a fixed direction, as the gypsy's mother said, as if he were heading to some specific place where he planned to leave the last chassis. Alone and probably of his own will, he dragged that truck chassis until he died, strangled on the last slope that separated the town from the cemetery. It was never known whether that was a suicide driven by the Dictator, a failed attempt at freedom, or both, but no one ever compared him to a person again, because in the town no one had ever wanted to take their own life just like that. In any case, what he did, he did because he was a donkey.

The only one who cried for the donkey was the mechanic's wife. She and the assistant dragged the little beast and buried it without speeches at the edge of town. Ramabad remembered them—sad and melancholic—walking far away on a rather deserted street, when Calataid's long night hadn't yet ended and a dark cloud of dust covered the highest part of the sky, leaving a still clear twilight on the horizon. They looked like three living bundles—he said—moving in the middle of a cosmic bonfire, but one of them was dead, and I carried it by one leg. Why is the Lord so unfair? the woman lamented, but no one ever knew for sure if she was referring to God or her husband. The woman cried like a Magdalene, and the fool accompanied her, crying even louder, as if he couldn't do anything without making a scene.

We buried the donkey in unsanctified ground, but under a wooden cross, which, some time later, was removed from the spot by the spirit of the mechanic. The excessive grief of the donkey's wife initially brought solidarity from some, and all kinds of comments later, when she began to periodically return to leave pieces of bitter chocolate scattered over the small mound of earth. Which, in the long run, brought a new tragedy, because the same chocolate that the donkey's spirit couldn't eat ended up attracting wild pigs who, unsatisfied with the dessert, overturned the table and dug up what was left of the deceased. And they ate it too.

The pigs didn't just eat donkeys when they were loose and hungry, but they had to be watched in cemeteries every time a Christian died. They had the habit of digging up anything that smelled bad, and a wooden coffin was no obstacle for their powerful snouts. A pig that escaped its owner and joined the group of wild ones never returned. They quickly developed a taste for it, if I may say so. And since there was a belief that bullets didn't harm their insensitive flesh from the corpses, they always tried to keep them as far away as possible, never attempting to approach them. It was better to let them run around the most distant dunes, with their snouts always stained with blood, than to have to figure out what to do if one of them happened to die near the town.

Athens, 2005

The masks

Shortly before dying, the old man had secured her a disability pension, and when she learned of her loneliness and her rights, she secluded herself in her room during the day and on the balcony at night. I loved her very much, and I believe she loved me just the same. Only, we shared a silent pact: we never spoke of our father, and I don't recall us ever uttering the name of the old woman, who was irremediably and voluntarily confined in a dark, unventilated room. We did everything by mutual agreement, without the need to speak directly about each thing. For example, I kept the saxophone and the old man's records, and she kept the telescope he used to see the craters of the moon, just as she saw the bacteria of hunger through the microscope. The bird also liked that instrument. As a child, he said he could see many countries on the moon, like in encyclopedias, some dominating others, empires crossing seas and mountains, subjugated islands and forgotten deserts, like ours. He would spend hours looking through that glass tube, until one of us went up to the balcony and interrupted him. He wanted to make me believe he could fly at night. In reality, she said, his wings had become very strong from the exercise of walking, and his legs didn't weigh him down like ours did. Then I would turn around and tell him not to make up stories, that the food was getting cold and I wasn't going to wait all night for him to come down. But she didn't want to stop exploring her moon. Until Dad died, and she no longer had anyone to believe a word she said. So she stayed up there and never came back. I know this well because she herself told me certain things that were happening in the town—like the mechanic's mistreatment of his donkey, forcing it to pull the cars he had piled up on his property—as if she could see them all from up there. Only she could know if the mechanic committed suicide upon seeing the black rooster for the second time or if his wife and the assistant killed him.

"Someone should do something," she would say to me, worried about the beatings the donkey was receiving and hoping I would decide to intervene. And since I wanted to keep her happy, I would cross the town and start talking to the mechanic, in the front yard, on purpose so she could see us. We would talk about the weather or anything else unimportant, mostly in a friendly tone, because I didn't like people but I didn't want to get on bad terms with anyone either.

Until one day I saw the creature tied to a post in the middle of the sun and felt what the bird must have felt. So I couldn't hold back and ended up demanding that the beast treat his donkey better. Only, I never imagined I'd get the response I got:

"And what's it to you?" he said. "Don't you think you're in no position to give moral advice to anyone?"

That time, the last time I spoke to the mechanic, we ended up arguing. I was arguing humanitarian reasons for the donkey, and he was defending his rights as the owner. The argument ended when the donkey's owner called his assistant, and the poor idiot approached with his hunched enormity and his clueless face.

"Yes, boss…"

"Get this musician out of the productive area."

The assistant did his best to impress me with his sleep-deprived, mean-looking face, full of pimples about to burst, while he repeated:

"Get out of the area, out of the area…" forgetting the rest.

The mechanic's assistant wasn't bad. I mean, he wouldn't have been able to kill his boss, no matter how pretty his wife was. He was a big guy and walked slowly, somewhat hunched and with his head forward, as if trying to hide his enormous height. He had straight, blond hair that fell over his eyes, like a golden helmet that shone in the sun and covered a lost gaze, probably the only one he had kept one day when he woke up without fully waking up and that showed how little he understood of the world around him, like someone in the middle of a heavy dream who never quite understands why sunflowers have eyes and farmers have blind seeds on their faces. When he was alone, he felt uncomfortable with himself and would move his head forward, as if he were listening to dance music without dancing. He always had one or two beetles in one of his fists. When no one was looking, he would open his hands, and the beetles would climb from the lowest finger to the highest, from the first to the second and back again, never tiring, until someone passed by and called him an idiot. Then the god of cycles would close his fists and hide the insects, frightened, as if he knew that spinning beetles was something dirty, indecent. Because there was also a rumor, I think only among the men of the town, that the idiot manipulated beetles on the advice or insistence of the priest, who intended to prevent him from masturbating on the sides of the roads, where women and even innocent maidens might pass. And since the idiot had been very well endowed by nature, like the donkey, he might give in to the temptation of committing some disgrace; to his monstrous temptation or to the innocent temptation of others. There were debates about the results: it was likely that the priest had succeeded, but in any case, it was a partial and very temporary success, because if it was always difficult for an intelligent man to control his own nature, it was probably even harder for the idiot.

The General could well have been my brother, some clandestine son of my unfaithful mother or my suicidal father. Everyone threw a stone at him whenever they could, like hens pecking without reason at chicks that walked with a limp or suffered from some visible deformity. But no one ever knew where he got the beetles, a search that would have puzzled even the most brilliant minds in the town. And, as I was saying, no one ever knew for sure what he did with them after making them dizzy. It was said that he killed them, squeezing them in his fists until the cavity of his enormous hands was nullified by the supernatural pressure of his idiocy, which undoubtedly justified the stones thrown at him by the younger ones. He was even known to have drowned some cats, as difficult as it is to drown cats in water. Granted: there was never any proof of this, not even the disappearance of a known beetle, but everyone said the same thing, and it's possible that he took pride in those lies, because the idiot must have sensed that people respected him for the same reason they threw stones at him. People respected the mechanic when he broke the donkey's ribs, so why would they bother with someone who enjoyed spinning beetles? Some even said that the idiot was rather innocent, harmless most of the time, though no one could guarantee anything when he exploded in rage, and for that reason, they had placed him with the mechanic so he could expend his energy dragging scrap metal from one place to another without any purpose. On the other hand, the mechanic needed an assistant who wasn't as intelligent as he was, given that he was a married man; and the one he got couldn't charge much, given that he was an idiot.

To me, he wasn't a bad guy, much less a murderer. The little violence he showed from time to time was a rare response to all the mistreatment he had received since he began to feel (if not understand, if anyone even understands) the world of normal people. I would say he was merely an innocent victim, and that was evident when he thought he was alone. When he was exhausted, he would sit on a car tire or lie face up on a fallen fuel tank, always with his beetles between his fingers and repeating, with a half-smile on his face: "From the knees down I'm standing, and from the knees up I'm lying down." Innocence didn't favor him, just as his intelligence didn't, diminished by some childhood mistreatment, or by prenatal misfortune, like mine or my sister's.

As for the donkey, I'll say it was the third major suspect in the death of its owner. As if it were responsible for my complaints, the mechanic had left it tied to a lamppost, day and night, with a bucket of water ten centimeters outside the circle drawn by the rope. For two nights in a row, I had to slip through the scrap metal to bring it water, but the donkey never moved from its position as a sad statue. It stayed like that, looking at me, resting on its crooked legs, as if instead of legs it were propped up on four crutches, with its enormous sad ears and white eye bags, its belly sagging more from a weak spine than from overfeeding, stubbornly refusing to try the water I offered, as if it no longer had any reason to trust any human and preferred to keep suffering from thirst rather than die poisoned. The last night I left the bucket against the post, risking that they would notice my intrusion, and the next day I forgot about the matter. Later, I found out, through the amused comment of the greengrocer, that the mechanic had put the donkey on a work penance, since, as everyone knows, these small beasts are very stubborn and grumpy, and often refuse to obey. Together with the idiot, they made it work double shifts, carrying pieces of cars back and forth, sometimes bleeding from its sides, where the axles and rusted sheets would dig in when the small beast couldn't move forward and, after the pull, the rope would yank it back, with even more hatred. The donkey divided the town in two: the few who looked unfavorably upon the mistreatment it received day after day, and the many who laughed at its crooked legs, twisted from the effort, and died of laughter at the braying it let out every now and then when the General of the Golden Helmet raised his stick as if it were a sword. The anonymous idea of placing an old fine Scottish wool hat on the donkey, with two holes for its enormous ears to stick out, was especially successful. The mechanic removed it as soon as he saw it from afar, furious because what was pulling a chassis was a donkey, not a human being. And since the mechanic wasn't willing to waste his time looking for the culprit of such a mockery, he unleashed all his rage on the already battered ribs of the donkey, which had to endure kick after kick for having lent its image to such an offense against the human species.

"Don't hit it, boss," said the General. "Look how it's crying."

To which the boss responded, shouting: "Don't be an idiot, don't you know that donkeys always do that? Every animal has its sound, and that doesn't mean it's crying. Hyenas go ha-ha when they fight, and that doesn't mean they're laughing. You'll see that if I hit it every time it brays, it'll lose the habit."

Over time, the idea took hold that the donkey had birth defects and, probably, was of a bad breed. It was compared to the other animals, and it was noted that, unlike each of the dogs, horses, and even cats, it was the only one that resisted obeying the mechanic. Therefore, it wasn't wrong for him to want to assert himself, just as a homeowner asserts himself over the ferocity of his dog, the trampling of his horse, or the whims of his wife. Of course, "asserting himself" didn't mean beating it all day, but quite the opposite: a man who has to resort to violence to earn respect is being resisted in some way. Violence could only be a temporary measure. However, the temporary seemed at some point to have no end, and this began to worry the town, which started to suspect that the donkey was incapable of understanding the message and, little by little, the laughter turned into irritation.

You might wonder why someone could hate a donkey so much. Especially because it was incapable of kicking back at anyone. Its sad face and its nature as a peaceful creature inspired both pity and anger at the same time, because one couldn't understand how it was able to endure day after day, blow after blow, without taking any action, like any person would.

The one who knew why the mechanic hated the donkey so much was the bird, though I never gave much credence to his enigmatic statements. I was wrong.

"The blond guy is bothered by the donkey's size," said the bird one night when we crossed paths in the hallway.

"The size...?"

"The man can't handle his wife, and she humiliates him by comparing him to the donkey. Don't make that face. That beast doesn't just beat the donkey; he beats his wife too. If the priest allowed him to divorce, she'd leave with the donkey."

"Isn't it that you like his wife, like everyone else?" I asked; but he must not have liked my attitude at all, because he turned on his right heel and went into his room.

Who knows if there was any truth to all this, if the bird was making up stories or finding out things that an ordinary passerby couldn't.

The only certain thing is that the donkey spent entire days moving tons of metal, pulling and enduring the mechanic's lashes, without braying in the end, which still didn't save it from the usual punishment. Until it was seen one midday, during siesta, with a rope around its neck and dragging a piece of a car down the path of the madwomen. More than one person got up from their siesta, intrigued by the mysterious noise the metal carcass made on the cobblestones, and saw the donkey walking, slowly and without rest.

"It finally learned to pull the metal without braying, damn it," someone said from a window. "But look how much trouble that son of a bitch gave us!"

At first, some laughed and went back to their homes to talk about what they had seen: that donkey was like a person, they said. Over time, and whenever silence threatened to take over a gathering, people would bring up the donkey again; the game was to attribute human intentions to it and compete in tests that proved it had been the best donkey the town had ever had in its entire history. A rare, abnormal case.

But while the donkey was alive, it annoyed everyone. Even the priest, who was Franciscan to about thirty percent. He stopped defending it when the General showed up one day at the church door, riding on it.

"Can you tell me where you're going, son?" was the priest's question, as he intercepted the idiot before he could enter the house of God with the beast in tow.

"Me, Father?"

"Who else do you think I'm talking to?"

"Yes, it's true," said the General, flashing his beautiful teeth and nodding his head as if he were confirming something all along.

"So?"

"So what, Father?"

"I'll repeat the question, more slowly, to see if you can answer it: what are you doing on top of that donkey, with both feet on the steps of my church?"

"I don't know, Father."

"How is it possible to do things without knowing what you're doing! When one doesn't know what they're doing, they stay still, do you understand, son?"

"Yes, Father, I understand, I stay still, like when I think about the patron saint and I touch myself down here, Father, and I don't know why I do it, yes."

"Alright, alright, alright, that's enough," the priest quickly interjected. "I already told you that stays between the two of us. You don't have to repeat it! That's not good, how many times do I have to tell you? Memorize what I say and don't repeat it. Do you want the whole town to find out what you do? Do you know what they'll say?"

"I don't know, Father."

"They'll say you're becoming more like the donkey every day!"

"Yes, it's true… It always happens to me, Father. I'm so forgetful…"

"Please, son, leave here, after taking off that crown of thorns, before more people see you."

"Yes, Father. I'm so absent-minded. That's it, absent-minded. I got on the donkey to take a little ride, and it brought me here on its own. If you don't stop it, Father, it'll go right into the temple with me and all."

Other stories about the donkey were better adorned with human attributes, which it surely didn't know or despised. The truth is, the time it was seen climbing the path of the madwomen, it was alone and with a clear destination, according to the gypsy's mother, as if it were heading to a specific place where it planned to leave the last chassis. Alone and probably of its own will, it dragged that truck chassis until it died, strangled on the last slope that separated the town from the desert. And it was never known whether that was a suicide or a failed attempt at freedom or both, but no one ever compared it to a person again, because in the town no one had ever wanted to take their own life just like that. In any case, what it did, it did as a donkey—the bird told me before taking flight, not without irony and preempting the town's comments.

Not long after, the mechanic was found hanged, with two or three bruises that were enough to classify the case as a homicide. The donkey could no longer be blamed, and since the possibility also offended the honor of the feminine nature, no one even mentioned the name of the unfortunate widow, who had cried for five days and five nights over the grave of the little beast without shedding a single tear for her husband. The woman also had visible signs of having been beaten, but in her case, it didn't attract anyone's attention, as the origin of the marks was well known. Nor did they point fingers at the assistant for long, a fact that, while surprising at first glance, a deeper analysis reveals that the townspeople never considered him a danger, but rather an aesthetic inconvenience.

So the only candidate for the position of murderer—at least on an interim basis—was me, the jazz musician. They had seen me arguing with the mechanic a few days before the suicide, and that incident was enough for a town that cared less about the truth than its own peace. And what could suit the people better than to disguise a suicide and, in the process, get rid of the trumpet player?

Two days after the mechanic's death, an Extraordinary Assembly was held at the Libertad club. Of course, I didn't attend, though unexcused absences were always frowned upon and, probably, that cost me dearly. In any case, that same night I learned of the Grand Resolution when they entered my house and practically dragged me out of bed.

"Get dressed," said a man with a mustache whom I couldn't quite identify.

"What's going on?" I said. "How did you get in here?"

"Get dressed quickly. Don't make us wait."

I dressed as they demanded. Like in a dream where you're drowning and can't move your arms or legs, I let myself be carried along by the intruders' orders. When I stepped into the hallway, I could see a dozen more people waiting downstairs in the living room. I wanted to approach my mother's door to tell her there were people in the house and that they intended to take me away. But a man dressed as a frog stopped me:

"Keep moving that way," he said. "Your mother is sleeping right now."

Later, I learned that they hadn't found enough evidence to blame me for the mechanic's suicide, but they had still found a way to punish me as they had long wanted to do. In a makeshift barracks in an abandoned estate on the outskirts of town, they informed me that the Assembly had resolved to execute the bartender's murderer, to set an example and leave no doubt about the peaceful customs of the town, carefully preserved for a century and a half and criminally disrupted by a stateless man.

"The murderer will die by blows of iron. That was the fairest method the Assembly resolved: an eye for an eye and a tooth for a tooth."

"Don't even tell me," I said, almost paralyzed with fear.

"You must know this now, as you have been chosen to carry out the Resolution."

"Chosen in absentia?"

"That's right. You missed the chance to vote."

I don't remember exactly what I said. I don't remember a single word. I got nervous and started shouting, insulting. I wanted to gouge out the priest's eyes, and all I could do was spit in his face. Or was it the colonel's face? It was a stubborn face, hypocritical, but I couldn't discern the degree of arrogance or cowardice that moved his muscles to compose an expression of rage and disgust.

"The Assembly's resolutions are not to be questioned. Do you dare to doubt the legitimacy of a democratic body like ours? Have you not benefited, since your eyes first opened to the light, from that very institution of the people? And now, citing personal convenience, do you intend to disregard it?"

"I'm a foreigner where I was born. I'll leave at dawn."

"This isn't ancient Rome, young man," said the mustached man in uniform; he also smelled of urine. "The same law applies to every living being that sets foot on our soil: *our* Law."

There was a lack of light and an excess of shadows, moving like restless souls on a peeling wall, so high it seemed as if that estate had once been the residence of giants, extinct in a distant time, or of dwarves with great power and wealth.

"No one has ever dared to question the Assembly," someone said in a hoarse voice behind me.

"But there's always a heretic who, on the least expected day, tries to break the rules of good coexistence."

"Pride condemns you, son," said the priest, calmly, with that feigned and obligatory tone of voice that every profession imposes.

"Please," I shouted angrily, "don't call me 'son.' You know very well I'm not your son and that you've probably never had one, despite advising the entire town on how to do it better."

I remember a hard blow to the mouth that left me dazed. Then, walking with rifles pressed into my ribs, to the island.

The island, as the colonel had called it, was more of a water pit, almost dry. And there I spent days and nights, my back pressed against the damp wall, walking in a circle a meter and a half in diameter to not lose strength when the time came to leave. Down there, in the deepest part of the earth, I had time and silence to think—as the colonel had asked me—about the reasons why the townspeople despised me so much. I concluded that it all stemmed from my bad appearance: my bulging, misshapen forehead had given me, since childhood, the profile of a buffalo, which only served to scare children and disturb the sight of adults, who said it grew year after year due to the inhuman effort of blowing the saxophone. For others, my forehead was the result of a difficult birth, as they had to use forceps to pull me from my mother's womb, leaving marks on my skull until I was five. For others, the difficulty of my birth was solely due to the exaggerated size of my head at the moment of gestation, which meant it was a genetic accident, the consequence of an addiction of one of my parents, or, quite simply, divine punishment. There were always disagreements and groups of supporters who backed one theory or the other. But if I may offer my opinion, I believe this forehead of mine only served to remind me, from the moment I gained reason, that I was different from others. A fact I tried to mitigate in my adolescence by tightly wrapping my head with a bandage at night, which never resulted in a reduction of the perimeter of my forehead but, rather, only served to wake me every morning with terrible headaches. Then I would measure the circumference of my skull with a tape measure and, with disappointment, confirm that the bandages did nothing to reduce its dimensions—quite the opposite: they increased them, making them even more prominent with the red-purple hue of skin punished by the useless pressure of the cloth. For a while, I made some effort to broaden my shoulders, to somewhat disguise the disproportion of my shadow—another useless and exhausting task, needless to say.

To make matters worse, failing at this art of reducing my head made me easily irritable. Which, in turn, gave my mother reason to tell everyone that the growth of my forehead didn't increase my intelligence but rather diminished it, or at least didn't allow it to flourish. I heard her say this a couple of times, not in a mocking tone, I know, but with sadness, during one of those long afternoons I spent with my ear pressed against the door of my room, leaving my greasy profile on the wood, day after day, trying to overhear the conversations of the visitors who came to her dark room and whom I always preferred to avoid whenever I could. I didn't want to see the visitors because I despised them and because seeing them meant exposing myself to being seen. Now, to be fair, it couldn't have been easy for my poor mother to have two children like my sister and me. After all, she had made us (with some participation from my late father), and all our flaws fell on her. My brother was handsome, but he lacked legs; and I, though I didn't have the body of an athlete, had an excess of head no matter how you looked at it.

Even in photos, the bird always had the upper hand. I say this with affection; I loved the bird very much, immensely. I was never jealous of him or anything like that, even though he was more handsome than I was, even though the mechanic's wife would look at her when she stood by the window and not at me as I walked past their house. The bird was well-proportioned and had a certain air of a movie star. Besides, it wasn't his fault that photographers were always interested in the upper parts of the body. It's understandable: social life unfolds almost exclusively in the upper hemisphere of the human body. In the head, one has all the senses concentrated and almost all of one's psychic life, including sex.

The bird wouldn't have needed legs if he hadn't fallen in love with the mechanic's wife.

As a child, I thought that the two of us could have made one normal person. And it wasn't just my idea: one night I heard my own mother saying to someone, "from two, I could have made one good one." It's true that the body is always precarious and a minority part of a human being; but the old women in the town wouldn't have been able to understand that. Age and stupid experience didn't matter; this defect of mine was enough to provoke terrible disgust in anyone who saw me on the street. Some women would even cross to the other sidewalk or make the sign of the cross if they were pregnant, as if I could infect them with my ugliness. And since they couldn't blame me for something I was born with, they blamed me for what I had acquired later: the habit of playing the saxophone like a madman.

And so I spent days and nights turning over my own existence, until the day of the execution arrived, and they hauled me up tied with several ropes, not only because I no longer had the strength to stand on my own, but because I had already decided to die.

From there, they took me in a jeep to the square where the town had gathered. The fleeting relief I had felt upon leaving ended when I heard the crowd murmuring in the distance. It was as if a heavy corn grinder had been placed on my head and turned on at that moment. I could feel the teeth of the wheel catching the kernels and crushing them, making that characteristic crunching sound that no one knows anymore.

In the square, an official placed a wood-chopping axe in my hands and pointed the way. In the center was the murderer, lying on the ground and wrapped in a black cloth.

"Let's get this over with once and for all," the man said and walked away.

To one side, but very close by, a group of women murmured the same words the priest had spoken at the mouth of the well. Or at least they did so with the same tone, grave and contrite. And the corn grinder began to turn again, bursting the kernels (*"...forgive us our sins..."*) while the murderer writhed in the middle, emitting groans that couldn't be heard clearly because a cloth filled his mouth.

Pushing through the crowd, the mayor drew a line in the dirt with a stake and delivered his awaited speech, this time shorter than usual:

"Those who stand on the side of Justice, on this side, and those who do not, on the other."

There was some timid protest, but eventually everyone moved to "this side," meaning the murderer and I were left on the other.

"You have nothing to fear," the pastor said. "Fulfill your duty as a citizen and cross the line. Your children will thank you one day."

"Come on, we don't have all night! We're freezing!"

I carried out the order. I struck the murderer with the back of the axe. I didn't want to cut him, I didn't want to feel the blade on his flesh, I didn't want to see blood. I just wanted him to stop moving, like a fish out of water. I just wanted to shorten the torment of someone who knew they were going to die, sooner or later, in the midst of an excited and gleeful crowd.

"Kill him, kill him now!"

I struck him again, this time a little harder than before.

"Divine! Kill me too!" a woman shouted, touching her breasts.

"That's it, boy, kill him now," they all shouted at once.

"Kill him!" one.

"I knew you wouldn't let us down," another.

"He's one of us," and yet another.

But the murderer refused to die. I struck him several times on the back, and he wouldn't die. There was always some movement in some part of that black bag. And I, who was incapable of ending his pain. On the contrary, my clumsiness only served to prolong his agony.

"Divine!" the woman with the enormous breasts kept shouting. "Don't rush so much."

"Yes, finish him off already," another pleaded.

"In the head!"

"In the head, further up."

"That's it, in the head."

Without a doubt, it was a good idea. In the commotion, it hadn't occurred to me. I should have started there, with a single, precise blow. That would have been the best way to spare him so much pain.

"Finish him, finish him!"

It was in the head. Only then did he stop writhing, and the crowd erupted in joy.

When the shouting had died down and the crowd began to disperse, I approached the murderer and unwrapped him until his face was revealed. He was wearing the bird suit. They had caught him like that or forced him to put it on, to end not only the murderer of the mechanic but, above all, the myth of the bird, which by then had surely become confused with the black rooster, of whom it was said that seeing him twice would cause a heart attack.

His eyes barely moved to wipe away the blood that prevented him from seeing me. "Don't suffer, brother," he said to me, "I killed him. It was me. Someone had to do it."

And he blinked no more.

But I know the mechanic killed himself, because I saw him climb the tree, the same tree as the donkey, because he couldn't bear to see me twice in the bird suit.

Tacuarembó, 2001

The First Man

*Reality is the madness
that remains
and madness is reality
that fades away*

Dr. Uriburu had returned one night from a clandestine healing house in Gitanera with a story he never revealed in his lifetime. According to him, he hadn't gone there in search of women but for a camel driver named Ibrahim who deceived him by selling him false translations from Arabic. One of these stories "The First Man"—which the doctor tweaked in its syntax, came from a column in the cisterns of Garama. As he had explained in other pages, these columns were written in Greek and Latin, in the form of a tight spiral that covered the entire shaft like a ribbon, from top to bottom.

According to this story, there was a time when men and women populated the world without knowing why they were born and died, like everything else. In reality, they used to see dead animals, trees struck by lightning, fallen brothers, and parents in agony. But these examples were not overwhelming enough to make them fear their own end. They mourned their dead, but the idea of disappearing did not frighten them.

One day, one of them had an extraordinary idea, seemingly inconceivable: he himself, who had seen a brother die, was also going to die. For many days he was sad, sitting on a stone by the river's edge. He had begun to contemplate his reflection in the river's mirror (when rivers still existed) and later lost himself in the contemplation of the trees, the sky above him, the sun setting behind the mountain's silhouette, and the stars. With the rise of the new sun, his situation did not improve.

He remained sad, deeply sad, and did not know why. It was simple; he was sad because he had discovered that death awaited him at the crossroads of some path. But for someone who had lived thirty years without knowing it, it was still a dark discovery. He barely had the words to explain this idea. That is, it took him even longer to understand that every path led to the same point. He told himself that this place was always sad, because although it was the common point of all paths, he would always arrive there alone. Then he understood why people cried when a loved one departed for the stars, so far away that they could never see them again.

After several days of wandering through the solitude of the desert (when the desert was not yet deadly for a man alone), he conceived a new and inevitable idea: if he told the others why he was in this state of sorrow, surely he would stop suffering. Or his suffering would not be so heavy. He had discovered that a man cannot bear such a heavy revelation alone, that he must share it with others, since they too shared the same fate. He discovered that, for this reason, others are, in some way, oneself.

Then he smiled, for the first time since that terrible day, and climbed up to the village. A column of smoke showed him the way. Beneath that column, he knew that other men and women (those other forms of himself) were roasting a wild boar.

"A dead boar," he thought, momentarily afraid.

On the way, he met a young man playing with a goose feather and felt he could not wait to reach the village to tell what had happened to him.

At first, the young man with the feather did not understand, as he had always thought that something happens when it occurs outside, like a bird struck down by a spear or a storm that throws fire upon the mountain. But how could something happen inside a person that was not just the beating of the heart?

The man understood that the young man had not understood and hurried to reach the village.

The next day, the young man with the feather, who had spent the night in the meadow, arrived at the village and learned that the man who had told him the strangest and most unforgettable story of his life had been killed. Or rather, he had been sacrificed to the new gods of the mountain. He also learned that they had killed him for something he knew, for something he had discovered by himself at the river, or who knows when, as they told him. Then the young man felt so afraid that he fled in despair, now aware that he possessed something that men either wanted or despised. And as he fled, he also knew that this something was not a stone, nor a ghost, nor a demon, but something he had learned, something he had discovered and carried within him somewhere.

He tried to remember what it was that so terrified the village and recalled what had happened to the first man. He remembered that the man knew he was going to die, just as it happened the next day. The man had predicted it, so it was true.

However, something even more terrible or marvelous had occurred: the young man with the feather also knew that the first man was going to die, without a doubt, long before the people of the village told him. He had no reason to doubt it, because at that time, lies did not exist.

Then he could no longer rid himself of that idea, and the idea began to spread like an epidemic: not only did he know that he was going to die, but so were all the others, in one way or another, sooner or later. The new, terrible thing was not so much death as the awareness of carrying it within since that day.

The young man continued to flee, and every time he met someone on the road who asked why he was running, he told this story, because he had not yet learned to lie. And so, the idea that we will all die someday took such a strong hold on everyone and spread so easily that soon there was no one left on earth who did not know it.

For centuries, men sought solace for their deepest anguish, but all answers seemed small in the face of death. Until someone, no one knows who, discovered the truth. And since they saw that it served as an answer to the fears of the first man, they defended it with their blood and the blood of others, first, and with lies afterward.

Athens, 2004

In the name of the supreme good

On the sixth or seventh night of confinement, just as the doctor had predicted, the plague spots disappeared. When they brought him up that dark afternoon, and we saw that this time the prisoner was clean, we immediately proceeded to carry out the democratic mandate of the jury.

The weather had worsened. An impossible climate settled over the Aurora desert for three days. A freezing wind blew from the north, carrying shards of ice that stung the skin of the face. Down in the cistern, Santoro had not noticed this change. But outside, the cold was unbearable. Perhaps this phenomenon had been one of the reasons why things escalated. The wait in the square was beginning to make people impatient; they, and we too, were at risk of catching a new epidemic.

They took Santoro to the Plaza Matriz in a closed cart, guarded by two boys he did not know. They were in uniform. On their faces, traces of a very recent childhood could still be seen, masked by a stern expression they must have copied from some experienced ensign who had taught them to be men and to love their homeland with fanatical obedience. Their eyes reflected all the pride of mercenaries who had not yet died.

The entire town had gathered in the square. The relief he had begun to feel upon leaving Abel's tower ended when he heard the crowd murmuring in the distance. It was as if a heavy corn grinder had been placed on his head and had just been set in motion.

Once in the square, they pushed him to the center and untied his hands. The new altar boy said a phrase in Latin that Santoro did not understand. Then an official in a blue uniform placed a wood-chopping axe in his hands and pointed the way. In the center, they had built a wooden platform. It smelled of fresh wood. Above was the murderer, writhing, wrapped in a black cloth.

"Let's get this over with once and for all," the man said and stepped back.

Santoro made a gesture of disapproval; or perhaps fear. He took the axe but let it fall to the ground. A general expression of annoyance was felt, though few words were spoken. To one side, but very close by, a group of women murmured a prayer, perhaps a rosary in Latin. At first, few recognized them by their long, dark dresses. They were not the Teresian nuns, for the holy women of the convent never left their prayers. They probably did not know that the mystery of Major Augusto had already been solved (they probably did not know that Major Augusto had been murdered, much less that obscene rumors about his daughter were being whispered).

It was later discovered that the women belonged to a splinter group of Pastor George Ruth Guerrero's church and, despite their Protestant vows, had found in the study of Latin a path to the origin of the true faith.

But in Santoro's misshapen head, these incomprehensible words bounced around without finding meaning. He looked to the sides and saw a boundless crowd, filling every corner of the square and the streets and alleys that led there. They were not shouting, but they roared like the sea he had seen in a movie days before. The corn grinder began to turn again, bursting the kernels as the murderer writhed in the center, emitting muffled groans because a cloth filled his mouth.

Noticing the prisoner's incipient disobedience, the bailiff made his way through the crowd to the center. With a stake, he drew an almost imaginary line on the worn ground of the square and said:

"Those who are on the side of justice, on this side, and those who are not, on the other."

There was some timid protest, but in the end, everyone stood "on this side." That is, the murderer and Santoro were left on the other.

"You have nothing to fear," Aquines Moria tried to console him. "Fulfill your duty as a citizen and cross the line." Your children will be grateful one day. Thus, all your sins and the sins of your fathers will be paid for.

"Come on, we don't have all night! We're freezing!"

He fulfilled his duty. He struck the murderer with the back of the axe. He didn't want to cut him, he didn't want to feel the blade on flesh, he didn't want to see blood. He just wanted him to stop moving, like a fish out of water. He just wanted to shorten the torment of someone who knew they were going to die, sooner or later, in the midst of an excited and gleeful crowd.

"Kill him, kill him once and for all!"

He struck again, this time a little harder than before.

"Divine! Kill me too!" shouted a woman, touching her breasts.

"That's it, my rooster, kill him once and for all," they all shouted at once.

"Kill him!" one.

"I knew you wouldn't let us down," another.

"He's one of ours," and yet another.

He kept hitting the black bag with force, but it was no use. There was no way it would stay still.

"Divine!" the woman with the enormous breasts kept shouting. "Don't rush so much."

"Yes, finish him once and for all," another pleaded.

"In the head!"

"In the skull, right there."

"That's it, in the head."

Without a doubt, it was a good idea. In the commotion, it hadn't occurred to him. He should have started there, with a single, precise blow. That would have been the best way to spare him so much pain.

"Finish him, finish him!"

It was in the head. Only then did he stop writhing, and the crowd jumped for joy.

Santoro was senseless for a long time. When the shouting subsided, like a sandstorm retreating, Santoro approached the murderer and pulled him out of the bag. He was wearing the bird suit. They had caught him like that or forced him to put it on, to not only finish off the murderer of Major Augusto but, above all, to end the myth of the avenging bird; a myth that by then had surely become confused with the black rooster, which, it was said, could not be seen twice without dying of a heart attack.

His eyes barely moved to wipe away the blood that wouldn't let him see.

"Don't suffer, brother," said the bird. "I killed Major Augusto. Someone had to do it…"

He was shattered. He wanted to say something, something important, something that should matter more to Santoro than to the bird (or so it seemed to Santoro). But his face remained in a kind of thoughtful smile. And he blinked no more.

From that day on, everything slowly returned to order in Aurora. Santero, the madman with the trumpet, sat outside the walls waiting for the train and remained there like a beggar. Secretly, everyone knew what he was waiting for, and, also in secret, everyone awaited the appearance of the train, one last time. Meanwhile, Santoro proclaimed that the desert would bury the cursed city. They forgave this repeated offense because he was mad, because his days were numbered, and because they finally recognized that Evita, the great dune, was beginning to overflow

Santiago's wall. The next sandstorm—Santoro said—the next sandstorm would forget the holy city. Then, despicable humanity would never learn of its proud existence, of its heroic mission on earth.

The following night, some followers of the bird whispered, in a corner of the triangular plaza of San Patricio, about the day of the judgment. They remembered how their own brother had killed him with an axe, severing his legs from the rest of his body. And some even said that before dying, just before taking flight, the bird had recited:

> *Reality is the madness*
> *That endures so vast*
> *And Madness, the reality*
> *That fades too fast*

And like a curse, they continued to recall other verses. No one knows who were the first to preserve the events of the Restoration and the forbidden verses of Aurora. Not even, no one knew if some verses had been remembered the night after the execution or if they were born from the murmuring mouths of the new reciters. But in any case, they said they were the verses of the bird, and their virtue lay in having continued to be written many years after his death. Not beyond Aurora, because those who tried drowned in the desert that, along with its walls of superhuman thickness, protects the Holy City.

Somewhere in the world, September 2007

Persistence of Joy

Around those days, Agadir had an encounter, initially insignificant and almost routine, that made him think about the thorny exercise of forgetting. It was a late afternoon as he walked along the Empedrada, near the gate of the cemetery. The wind had picked up and was shaking the tops of the palm trees. The sand rose up to his knees, erasing the stones of the avenue in that almost forgotten part of the city, announcing another storm and a new overflow of the great dune over the southern wall that protected the city. Yet, people went about their daily shopping and swept the sidewalks as if it would make any difference.

Turning onto San Jorge, Agadir saw a procession of faithful approaching, dressed in faded black and carrying banners and red flags with golden inscriptions. He tried to read them but could barely open his eyes. They turned onto Empedrada and passed in front of Agadir as if he didn't exist. Their gaze was unwavering, and they marched like an army indifferent to the force of the wind. Though he tried to look several times, he could hardly make out their faces. He didn't recognize anyone; a wave of sand hit him in the face.

He entered through San Jorge and then through Carmelita. In an alley where a donkey was taking shelter, he discovered one of the few World War II cars that had made it to Amarabad, abandoned since the days of independence, now half-buried in the sand and almost unrecognizable. Shortly after, as he passed under a narrow stone arch, he crossed paths with a woman. At first, he thought she was a beautiful young woman, with her slender figure wrapped in cloth and trying to escape the force of the wind. He looked into her eyes and saw an old or aged woman, surprised by the interest of the man approaching her.

She stopped and said to him:

"You, handsome man, carry a great sadness."

"What a talent," said Agadir, trying to move away.

"It's a talent the Lord gave me. Come, man," she insisted, following him with that tone typical of the gypsies from outside the walls, "let me tell your fortune."

"I already know my fortune," said Agadir. "If you have a bit of good luck to give me, I'll be grateful."

"I'll tell your future for twenty dinars."

"I'm not interested. Give me some good luck, and I'll give you ten dinars."

"Come on, good man, everyone wants to know their future."

"Not everyone."

"Give me twenty, and I'll tell you everything, absolutely everything. Come on, man. Let's see…"

She took his right hand. Her face was crossed with wrinkles, the kind of deep, well-defined wrinkles of people who have lived much of their lives outside the walls. The sand stuck to her mouth and eyes, but she looked as if nothing were wrong.

"You're going to die," she said bluntly.

"You don't say?" he replied. "Woman, we all know that. A few know when, but no one knows where."

"God knows where, and we fortune-tellers know when. Give me twenty dinars, and I'll tell you everything."

She took the money and studied the hand that had given it to her more closely, as if the previous statement had been in bold headlines and the details were in fine print:

"Let's see, good man, you're leaving us very soon. This year, by Christmas at the latest. You're going to die in your sleep. From one dream to the next, which is the best way."

"All that's in here? Look, I haven't even washed my hands yet. Couldn't it just be a bit of dirt? I mean, maybe a little smudge that could be mistaken for death…"

"I see everything here, and clearly."

"Dying, and dying soon, is within the realm of possibility. I'm no angel. Of course, dying in my sleep is something I hadn't thought about."

"If a fortune-teller tells you, it's not just probable. It's certain. Besides, I've been doing this for fifty years, and I know what I'm saying: *you're going to die*."

"At least sell me a bit of your good luck," said Agadir, a little nervous, inexplicably nervous, as if the sun and the temperature had suddenly dropped and a cold gust of wind had begun to blow. An hour earlier, he would have said that death was the long-awaited relief. But one grows old and nostalgic and begins to yearn for the present, all that one sees for the last time, like a traveler leaving a beloved home, a city, a country, knowing they won't return from exile. He looked toward the center: people walked bent forward, their heads wrapped in white cloth that the sand and wind were determined to unravel. It was time to seek shelter, not to stand on the Empedrada talking about the consequences of not doing so.

"I can't, good man," said the gypsy. "Luck is something I can't sell or give away. I don't have any left, and you can see that. But I can do something else. If you give me twenty more dinars, I can make you forget what I just told you." People don't like to know when they're going to die. It's one of the most valuable ignorances that keeps them alive and always striving for great endeavors. Tonight and the nights to come, you'll want to forget what I told you, and if I hadn't seen it in your hand, I wouldn't have said anything.

"A perfect deal," said Agadir. But, in some way, the fortune-teller had told him the truth without realizing it. He thought it was like when one retains a nagging worry about a duty they've forgotten to fulfill. I've forgotten something important, and I don't know what it is. It's like when one keeps the unease, the fear, the dread of a dream that disturbed them in the night but can no longer remember the next morning, at least not in detail, and yet it persists in a much worse way, because now it's a secret to which we've lost access.

"Surely a few blocks up," said Agadir, "today, yesterday, or last week, another fortune-teller did the same job, both things together, the revelation and the forgetting, because for days now I've been walking very sad, along this same street, and I don't know why. The worst has already happened to me long ago. The music isn't what it used to be, women no longer stir my heart. I eat and drink well every day, better than before. I've stopped seeking happiness. If you make me forget what you've told me, you won't free me from my sadness, I'll have twenty dinars less, and I won't know why I'm so sad. Now, if I know I'm going to die, at least my sadness is justified."

The fortune-teller muttered an indecipherable curse and disappeared into the clouds of sand.

Agadir had stopped seeking happiness. Then he smiled at fate, and sadness and death had no choice but to admit their defeat. They say that was joy.

Athens, 2003

The first death of
Ernest Hatuey

ON AN ASPHALT STREET covered by the dust that blurs everything, at the hour when the day divides between afternoon and night and the smells of the villages of Iraq become as intense as in the grain and spice shops of the Arabs in Manhattan, the convoy entered the ancient city without changing its pace. Through the small window of unit 16, Ernest saw the first houses with flat roofs and no lights inside pass by. He saw the same people as always, walking like gray, silent shadows, as if trying to exist as little as possible, just enough to return to their homes, or as if they didn't know any other way to live. He had grown accustomed to the houses and the streets, always blurred, as if they were an unfinished sketch, with no clear boundaries, no precise colors, nothing sharp that made that city a city and those people concrete men and women rather than characters from old children's stories.

Between 17:00 and 17:15, an explosion lifted the unit marching ahead into the air. As the procedure for such occasions dictated, the units ahead that hadn't been affected didn't stop. The one in front of Hatuey slowed down to divert the damaged unit while a soldier opened fire on the natives who hadn't yet recovered from the stampede.

In the usual vertigo, heightened by the deafening blast, Ernest leaned out of the hatch and saw a man trying to lift a child. Somehow, he didn't know how, he had seen that man and that child a moment before the explosion. They were walking hand in hand. They were dressed more or less the same, without colors, in loose shirts and pants, white, gray, or simply dirty. At some point, the child began to run as if he had seen the Devil himself. He was barefoot. A few seconds later, the explosion occurred, and almost immediately, the burst of gunfire from the unit ahead.

Two comrades from Arizona died, though he never knew who. Perhaps he knew the name of the child who had fallen in the second burst. He remembered the shouts in Arabic from someone calling him. He remembered the child's scream and, above all, he remembered, like an eternal curse, the silence that had followed that raw expression of pain or fear. The man shouted *Johef*, or *Yohef*, or *Youssef*. It was a shout like a vomit, as if in one of those names he was vomiting out his entire life in that land cursed by God, he thought. The vomit stretched into the *e*, into the last *e* that dragged into a snore that then choked in the *f*. *Yousseeef*. He didn't know why, but this vowel had become something important in his life. Why did the vomit choke on that *e* that sometimes turned into an endless *i*? Why had those details stuck with him when there were more important things in the war? The man shouting must have been the father. Because only a father—he dared to think—could scream in a way that cut to the bone. Maybe he was shouting for the convoy to stop, he once admitted, completely drunk in a bar on Ocean Front Street in Jacksonville Beach. Maybe he was shouting for the soldiers to stop clearing the area before continuing the march, he omitted saying that afternoon, but he acknowledged it in an email he sent to his cousin Eduardo in San Francisco, just as he was leaving Hawaii on the tuna boat that would eventually take him to Japan.

He also admitted, in the same email, that when he heard the first scream, he almost stopped the Abrams. It would have been against regulations, which is why the unit continued on its planned route.

But the best reasons to forget didn't matter. Ernest couldn't shake that scream, the *e* and the man trying to lift something without a concrete shape. As if that had been the only casualty in the entire war.

The child had been left behind, lying in a pool of blood. His father kept trying to lift him, but for some reason, he couldn't figure out how. Hatuey cursed him for it. Over and over, he had seen it in his dreams trying to lift that bundle tangled in a white or gray robe.

Ernest Hatuey was going to stop the M1 Abrams. He could have done it, even though it was against regulations. He could have done it, and he didn't. Nor could he know if the child had died in the explosion or under the tracks of the Abrams. And even though he had handled the situation correctly according to the rules and standards, even though he had seen many people die before and after that afternoon, that afternoon wasn't like any other—and only God and the Devil know why.

For the rest of his deployment in Iraq, Ernest Hatuey fulfilled his duties within the objective and the expected forms. In war, it's impossible to notice when something is wrong, so in the following months, he worked with discipline, waiting for the final return.

Finally, on Wednesday, March 21, 2007, he arrived at Hartsfield-Jackson Airport in Atlanta. When he took the metro from Terminal B to T, he wanted to think about Claudia, about his parents. He wanted to feel the same anxiety as his comrades.

Next stop, concourse C... C as in Charlie...

He knew they were waiting for him. His father, excited but expressionless; his mother crying; and Claudia, the delicate butterfly who had escaped the Colombian paramilitaries almost ten years ago, nervous, as always, thin and unable to control so much anxiety, because for her, the world hung by a thread, and every detail of every event was a terrible threat.

He would have liked to feel nervous, but he couldn't. There were no strong emotions in his stomach, nor the tears he had imagined so many nights, lying on the bunk in the detachment, unable to sleep, with a cigarette occasionally lighting up the ceiling, like in Vietnam movies, recounting details about his mother and his dog, listening without much interest to the details of his comrades' mothers and dogs, listening to *Paint it Black* by the Rolling Stones to mask reality. Every time he recounted something about his almost forgotten life in San Juan, he traveled to the Caribbean and smelled the guavas, saw the grandmother's flowers that surrounded the water well and climbed the back wall, which he imagined as the last bastion of the fortress hiding a beautiful young woman kidnapped by pirates, never realizing that pirates didn't own castles but ships, their own and others'. And the coquí, of course, the coquí multiplied by a thousand on carless nights. Co-quí, co-quí… When Aunt Eulogia was dying in Orlando, her daughter played a recording of these little frogs in the hospital room. Two nurses had come in upon hearing the strange noise and took a while to understand that it was a recording, that the recording was of little frogs, and that the little frogs made the patient feel good. But Aunt Eulogia needed nothing more than silence and the coquís. She had smiled and, before dying, thanked her daughter for taking her back to Puerto Rico.

"*Hatuey, besides being a strange name, has a very creative memory,*" said Jesús, the Dominican ballplayer who slept in the bunk below.

"*Don't be ignorant,*" Hatuey replied, "*don't you know who Hatuey was?*"

He let himself be carried up one of the escalators. Then another. Two women were running breathlessly to catch their flight.

"*I know,*" Carlos had answered from the darkness, "*it's a Cuban malt brand. A Chilean friend of mine loved drinking malt, and the only place he could get it was at a Cuban restaurant in West Palm Beach, full of Cuban girls, though they were born in America. My friend, who liked Che Guevara more than the Miami mafia, would go there to eat Cuban empanadas because the Yankees had no idea what malt was. The worst part was that he ended up falling in love with one of those girls, and I think they even got married.*"

"*I don't want to know what happened after that.*"

"*Now that I think about it, it had an Indian on the label. The malt.*"

"*And the cigars, the Cohibas, and all that. But the truth is, it's a Taíno Indian, the first rebel of America.*"

Next stop, concourse T… T as in tango…

But all of that had been before Fallujah. Before Fallujah, the horrors of war were just that; they were the horrors of war that happened every day to someone who was still alive.

Without realizing it, he suddenly found himself walking at a measured pace in a line that meandered through the airport. *I see a red door and I want it painted black.* A blonde woman with a small flag in one hand led the line of soldiers and guided them through the different waiting areas so the heroes could receive the welcome they deserved. *No colors anymore I want them to turn black.* A crowd of unfamiliar faces, some disheveled, as was customary, was there to cheer them on. He barely saw two or three men and a woman reading the newspaper or drinking coffee, with an indifference that seemed deliberate to Hatuey. He didn't even feel hatred or anger toward those ungrateful people. He almost understood them. He almost wished one of them would stand up and say something, maybe an insult, but something that would end that agony of heroes. He could see in their faces all the patriotic passion that he, Ernest Hatuey, had lost in the war. *I see the girls walk by dressed in their summer clothes...* He held no grudge against the country he represented. His resentment came from somewhere else, but the noise of the applause didn't even let him understand to the slightest degree where that resentment came from, the one that made him despise that fat woman whose face was red from clapping so much, or that old man who shouted, *"welcome, welcome!"*

From all these signs, he knew he was sick or something wasn't right. A doctor would explain to him years later that there is a soldier syndrome that transfers all their frustrations and traumatic experiences to the authorities who had sent them to war, and that this could be cured by forgiving and opening a dialogue with those who, at the time, had to make the decision that ultimately ended up affecting the life of the renegade soldier. But Hatuey discovered, to his complete surprise, that there were many comrades in the same situation, at least far more than any of them could admit.

As he walked in silence, dragging those sand-colored boots from the East across the shiny floor—boots he was supposed to keep as the greatest trophy of his life—Ernest kept waiting for the emotion to well up in his eyes as he went through the welcoming ceremony. All his comrades had been anxious from the moment they spotted the shores of the United States until the very last minute.

When the martyrdom of the welcome parade ended, they all threw themselves into the arms of their parents and their wives. Some even had small children. He felt envy for those little children, running like crazy to throw themselves into the arms of their absent father, who had been in a mysterious land, in an ungrateful distant country that had devoured so many of those suffering heroes. And thanks to them, their children were now free.

Ernest Hatuey tried to do the same. When he saw his parents and Claudia with tears streaming down their faces, he opened his arms and smiled, though his eyes didn't follow. He couldn't feel the emotion. Much less cry or squeeze a tear from those eyes dried out by the desert sand. Dried out, he thought, as if they were dead. He tried to fake emotion, but he couldn't.

There were his wife and his parents, and there he was doing what he was supposed to do: hugging them, telling them he was happy to be back. But all he could think about was getting home and lying down. It was as if a great weariness, after days of walking, had overtaken him for no reason.

At home, he found his dog Glory, the dog he had missed so much. There she was, nervous, jumping as high as her legs would allow. Ernest Hatuey knelt down and hugged her, trying to avoid the desperate licks of that little beast who hadn't understood a thing.

A few months after his return, the doctors diagnosed Ernest Hatuey with PTSD, that is, *post-traumatic stress disorder.* As they explained to him, no one yet knew why the same experiences have different effects on different people, or even on the same person. But at least all the rage against the strangers who had stayed behind and all the indifference toward his wife and his parents now had a name, and the doctors probably had some idea of how to alleviate a problem that had become chronic because it hadn't been treated in time, or so they said.

So, little by little, he came to realize that on that day, March 16, 2006, he had died in the explosion or shortly after, and his corpse had been left lying on a dusty street in Fallujah, in the hands of an unknown father, as unknown as the one Ernest himself had found upon his return in Atlanta, on a fall afternoon in 2007.

Jacksonville, 2011

He had other plans

Two years earlier I had separated from my little wife. It turned out that time ended up proving my in-laws right, who had said that with me their beloved daughter would starve, that because of me the princess had left the son of the Curbelos, the family who owned the wine shop near Buenaventura, and who eventually ended up hiring poor Lorena as a domestic servant, who didn't even look like she was from Chihuahua, as a very, very special favor, it was said, to my poor mother-in-law who had gone to beg them for alms for her daughter who was languishing in the misery of a dry land and an even more useless husband.

One day, just as I was returning from the struggle in the cornfield, all sweaty and thirsty, before I could even say "I'm here," poor Lorena told me she was going to accept the job the Curbelos had offered her in Buenaventura, that it was just for a while until things got better, and that she loved me, and would always love me, but that she also had to think about our son, that this wasn't a life, much less a future for a three-year-old boy who would soon have to start school, and that there was avocado and guacamole. She loved me so much and always would, but for me the suitcases and the sniffling child spoke louder than words.

Things speak for themselves, and when they need a lot of explanation, it's because someone is lying. I'm not saying my wife didn't love me, but it seemed like not enough to keep her from humiliating me to that point. The only thing that was clear to me was that she was going to work as a domestic in the house of the people who would have been her in-laws. The house that would have been hers, in a word, because in-laws, like everyone else, die one day, because it must be the law that one makes room for those who come after. Young Mr. Iván Curbelo Montenegro, who should have been called Monterrubio, like all the Curbelos, and who could have been her honorable husband, at least until a month ago, was engaged to an Italian woman of noble lineage, with a last name I don't remember but it was something like Prodi or Parodi, not very pretty but educated and wealthy, so I don't think poor Lorena could hook up with him again, out of convenience or nostalgia, or that she could cheat on me before hearing news of me in the United States, but for me it was humiliation enough that my child had to play on the carpet the Curbelo Montenegros walked on and that he didn't want to see me on weekends, that my wife had to live with the idea that her life could have been better with someone else, and that she had to tidy up every day all the closets she had lost thanks to a youthful whim, which had ruined her future with what you see here before you.

After she left me, I stayed in the little house with the old man, taking care of the land until I saved up enough money to head over here. I figured if I sent the three of them about three hundred dollars a month, I could still come back in five years. The before. I was going to return in a different way, with some dollars to pay off the old man's debts and start a new business, having seen where the truly rich live and not just pretentious people like the Curbelos. But the old man got sick right away, not long after Lorena left the house and I started thinking about coming over here. Suddenly, without warning, he realized he was going to be left alone. All alone and defeated. A failure himself, and swallowing the failure of his son, which must be several times worse than one's own failure, that bitter and disgusting thing that one day, sooner or later, one has to chew on in solitude so it doesn't infect the people one loves. So from the chaos of the little one and the lively conversation of his children every day at dinner time, the old man was going to pass into the final loneliness, the kind that always accompanies the elderly, no matter what they say or what their kind children promise. Have you ever promised something important to your parents? Yes? Yes? Well, you're out of luck. Parents keep their promises. Parents almost always keep their promises. Children almost never. *Never*, in a word. And that's why I'm here now. Maybe my old man got sick from the disappointment or from bad food, only God knows. What's certain is that he didn't even have the horse left to pull the cart that would take us to town the afternoon he felt sick, and he preferred to die in his bed. That afternoon, before

221

I went to work in the cornfield, he had said that my mother had died in that same bed and he wasn't going to be any less brave, because the old woman, who was watching from somewhere, didn't deserve it. I thought it was just words, nothing more. Sentimental old man stuff. But no. In reality, he didn't die in the same bed, as he would have wanted. He didn't even get that right. When I came back from cleaning the corn, I saw from a distance that the old man was standing at the door of the house, waiting for me. Then I realized. It's one of those things you know without knowing how you know. He didn't say anything, but I knew he had been waiting for me to say goodbye. When I hugged him, he collapsed on me and said, "Son, forgive me. I wanted to leave you something to help you and I couldn't. I'm so sorry, my boy," he said, and then he died, in my arms.

So as soon as a doctor from Nuevo Casas Grandes showed up to certify that the old man was officially dead from a heart attack, I took him to the riverbank where we always fished as kids, the four of us, mom, dad, my brother Lorenzo, and I, and I buried him there, under the little tree, in a half-broken secondhand coffin I had bought from the town gravedigger, an old drunk who recovered coffins when families downsized their deceased and resold them as if they weren't going to need them again, as if the rest of the family were immortal or something like that.

Afterward, I sold the few things that were left, the four milk cans, the cart without a horse, some gold rings of the old woman that I only then discovered my father had kept under the bed, some furniture still good for use, the doors and windows of the house before the creditors and lawyers caught wind of it. I spent the last week eating herbs and drinking liquor from some agaves that grew on their own near the old man's grave, and as soon as I could, I left for here. I had to haggle over the price for several days at the border because I didn't have all the money the coyotes charge, and there I was just one more, with nothing of all I've told you, because no one cares, just as I didn't care about other people's misfortunes. There I was just another little Indian, even though I'm not Indian at all except for the plaid shirt and the slightly short pants, because I had to save the new ones for looking for work in the land of the rich. In Ciudad Juárez, a buddy from Nuevo Casas Grandes covered the part I was missing, for nothing, because there are still good people in this world, and that's how I'm here. Life goes on for some, because the worst part is always carried by those of us who are still left, which only stops being true when we have a few tequilas.

My brother died trying to do what I'm doing now. He died walking through the desert of New Mexico. He probably didn't even have the luck of being buried with dignity. The ants ate him or the earth swallowed him. I don't say it as a reproach. After all, I know that everyone who could have accompanied him in the attempt was in the same boat, trying to survive and escape La Migra, thirst, the coyotes, and the damn mother. My dear mother died of grief a few months later. Five months later. Still, she held on for a long time, as the old man told me one evening when I found him lying on the side of the road leading out of town, drunk, with a gash on his forehead and harassed by some brats who were having fun singing *Ay, ay, ay, ay, sing and don't cry, because singing brings joy, cielito lindo, the hearts...* I almost killed one of those sons of bitches with a rock I threw, which thankfully didn't hit him just right. All that happened in '92.

My old man died of appendicitis. Appendicitis, peritonitis, or anguish. Who knows. Maybe even the doctor didn't know what my dear father died of, and he didn't care whether he wrote down heart attack, indigestion, or cirrhosis. What did it matter... As long as he gave some scientific name to someone else's misfortune, that was more than enough. That was his job, and he wanted to do it quickly to get out of there, out of that room that surely disgusted him or, at the very least, left him indifferent. The truth (that the old man had died of anguish, of sadness, of love, or of disappointment with life) didn't matter, and soon it would be buried along with that poor sack of flesh and bones that to me was still my father. Sometimes I think about all the gestures, all the grimaces that his poor face must have made from that day until it turned into a little pile of clean bones. At least I was able to bury him myself under a little tree older than all of us, under the watchful gaze of Lobito, his dog, who mourned him the most, because I knew how to hide it. I hid it, God knows why, because only Lobito and I attended the burial. So the old man finally rested near the stream at the back of the property, which wasn't even a property anymore because it was seized due to all the debts he had accumulated with the bank.

There was no hospital nearby, but the bank was like God: it was everywhere, and we prayed to it every day. All the previous year we had worked from sunup to sundown and from moonrise to moonset. We had worked like beasts, more than ever, but God and the Virgin didn't love us that much, so they never heard our prayers for a single drop of rain. We must have done something wrong, surely, we just didn't know what. The bank had promised to pay us for the seeds and tools in exchange for our work, but no one ever said that year not a single drop of rain would fall, and so the only thing that grew was our debt with the bank. Of course, the bank wasn't to blame for God not sending rain; we were to blame, and we had to pay for it. The debt and the old man's anguish piled up in his chest until the poor man doubled over in pain as soon as night fell. At first, wine eased it, but little by little, neither wine nor tequila nor any other lie we heard on the radio about how things were getting better in the country and all that could help. So as soon as the old man died I had no choice but to leave for good. If I sold, I'd be in debt. So I took Lobito to the Hernández's house, some good neighbors who lived a league away and were as indebted as I was, and I told them to make use of the old man's field while they could, before the men with the papers arrived. I told them they had my permission, even if it was just a moral one. I don't think anyone would dare move Dad's grave from where it is, because they're all good Christians. There may be people out there who despise life, but no one messes with death. So I left everything as it was and went. I said goodbye to every corner of the house and the field and left, sure I'd never return. I left without sorting out any papers. What for? I couldn't expect anything good from any papers. The poor and papers never get along.

Philadelphia, 2008

The Galician Suarez

One Thursday, the day after the coup d'état in Uruguay, old Suárez, the Galician who brought coffee every morning from the corner bar, said:

"And how do you expect me to be, Mr. Caballero? You already know. Good news for some and terribly bad for others. That's how it is when there's no democracy or when there are too many people who hate it. I asked the doorman how long he thought the military would stay, and he told me to start saying goodbye to Wilson and Zelmar. That they're done for. I asked if he was happy, and he asked me if I was a communist, you know? When someone asks you if you're a fascist or a communist, it's because things are really messed up. No, not at all, I said, I was just a Spanish republican. I told him *I was* just in case. And he told me to start looking for another homeland because this one wasn't working out for me either. To the Congo, he said, to the Congo. So today they gave me the coffee… They gave me that coffee, they gave it to me. Do you know what that means…? No, no… you're talking to me like a Uruguayan. In Argentina, it's the same. Here they say 'they gave me a coffee' to mean they scolded you, treated you like garbage, like that crazy doorman treated me. The thing is, you came here very young, Mr. Caballero. Back in Spain, the Francoists used to sing… (old Suárez shaped his mouth into an *O* and looked up at the ceiling, searching his memory):

> *…they say you're leaving, you're leaving*
> *and yet you never quite go*
> *to see that blonde they say*
> *you have in Valladolid…*
> *I'll give you*
> *I'll give you something*
> *I'll give you, beautiful girl*
> *something only I know: coffee!*

Old Suárez, with his unshaven beard and his gray eyebrows drooping over his eyes, looked at Don Jordi as if he couldn't understand why he didn't understand.

"Well, you heard it," he said. "I'll give you something, something only I know, *coffee!*"[*]

He looked at him again as if the office had suddenly darkened.

"The thing is," he said, sounding disappointed. "you're much younger than me, and I don't know if I'm doing the right thing by telling you, but when I was a young lad, I

---

[*] Coffe, *café*. In Francisco Franco's fascist regime in Spain, CAFE, "*Camaradas, Arriba Falange Española*" (Comrades, Long live the Spanish Phalanx).

worked making tiles, those same gray tiles with nine little gray squares on top, the ones you see everywhere here in the neighborhoods, and, well, I had to be a republican, and when we heard someone singing that coffee song outside the factory, it sent a chill down our spines because we knew that 'coffee' was their way of saying "Comrades, Up with the Spanish Phalanx"… And look at that, Mr. Caballero, the twists of life, I had to cross the entire ocean, just like you, and I started as a waiter at the Lugano's bar, so it's been over thirty years now that I've been carrying and serving coffee. And to top it all off, on the day after the worst day in this country, they give me coffee… and it's like there's no turning back now. At my age, there's no Congo that can save me, not even in my dreams.

Old Suárez turned, hunched over, toward the office door, and Don Jordi remembered the silence of his mother on the other side of the Atlantic.

"Don't be like that, Pepe," said Don Jordi. "None of this is your concern… Why worry about it?"

Jacksonville, 2011

Was so much cruelty necessary?

The lieutenant knew that María had allowed herself to be raped because she knew her son was hiding somewhere in the shed. Once, on a summer night, drenched in sweat on an unbearable pillow, he woke up with another one of his absurd ideas: María Fuentes de Ocampo had died pregnant with his child. For two or three consecutive days, he woke up in the early hours with the same thought. Then, he'd go out to the balcony for some fresh air, and everything would go back to normal. Until the next night.

"Was so much cruelty necessary?" asked an older Don Xico once, at the gun club in Montevideo.

On the TV, *Heidi* had started, but no one got up to change the channel.

"Of course it was," replied Colonel Rago, in his familiar hoarse Italian-New York accent, both ironic and surprised by such a question, like a believer doubting his minister's sermon. "We were at war. Or have you forgotten what Che Guevara did when he won in Cuba? He executed a bunch of people from the previous regime. That's what they would've done to us."

Grandpa
Tell me 'bout the good ol' days
Sometimes it feels like
This world's gone crazy

"Yes, that's what they would've done," someone confirmed from behind.

A silence fell over the dark room of the club. It was dusk, and no one got up to turn on the lights.

Grandpa
Take me back to yesterday
When the line between right and wrong
Didn't seem so hazy

"And why didn't we execute them too?" said Major Almeida y Laprida. "We would've saved ourselves all the rest..."

"We needed information. That's why," someone said from behind.

Did families really bow their heads to pray?
Did daddies really never go away?
Woah-oh, grandpa
Tell me 'bout the good ol' days.

Jacksonville, 2012

Reader's Digest

He thought he heard the double knock of a door knocker. But the building was empty at that hour, and there were no knockers on the modern glass doors. Without getting up, he swiveled in his chair and looked toward the door leading to the hallway. The bulletproof glass multiplied the silence and the indecipherable reflections, as if spaces were mixing at that moment like a deck of cards

"Who is it?" asked a frightened voice.

It was his mother's voice, drowned out by a crowd of footsteps that piled up at the entrance of the door.

"He's not here, I'm telling you..." insisted the voice.

That voice was still there. It wasn't a hallucination or a product of his imagination. It was his mother's voice, still murmuring, in a corner of 1939. More precisely, in the evening of Barcelona on February 9, 1939, the same day Juan Negrín crossed the border, a few hours after his father managed to start the Ford A, and just minutes before the Falangist boots entered his room.

Later, he heard his mother, utterly defeated, like any woman of her status at that time, speaking in codes and whispers with another woman dressed in black, that the cross and rosary his mother had sent from A Coruña, and which, by some dark intuition, she herself had hung in Jordi's room a few days earlier, had saved the family, or rather, what was left of the family, from an even greater misfortune.

Though he couldn't hear this last part; he only remembered it.

When he saw him for the last time in Barcelona, on that cold afternoon in 1939, his father was thirty-five years old. Jordi Caballero learned the exact date one summer day, almost sixty years later, lying on a beach on the Costa de Oro in Uruguay, reading a tiny article in Reader's Digest *Reader's digest* that talked about the preludes and premonitions of the Second World War. Something less than a page was dedicated to the Spanish Civil War. "To resist is to win." But England had betrayed the Republic by making a pact with the Falangists in exchange for ensuring that Menorca didn't fall into Italian hands. On February 9, the Reader said, President Negrín had crossed the border into France. It was then that he remembered his father's words. "At this moment, Negrín must be crossing the border."

He didn't remember the voice. He only remembered that this revelation was something important and probably dramatic. His mother, leaning on the kitchen table, had rested her forehead in her hand and stayed like that, without saying a word. Jordi was playing on the floor, or pretending to play with an empty matchbox—*fósforos*, as they called them in Uruguay—which had become a newspaper delivery truck, like his father's. What could all that mean for Mom? Resist, border, Negrín... To Jordi, that name sounded like the name of a gnome, a character from fairy tales with some attribute or a dark, ominous destiny. Negrín, the champion, Negrín, the jumper...

Sixty years later, Jordi had put the magazine down and left it on his chest while he looked at the flat horizon of the sea with surprised eyes. "At this moment Negrín must be crossing the border," he repeated several times. The last time, out loud.

Lucía, who was fifteen at the time, asked:

"What did you say, Dad?"

"Nothing, sweetheart," was the reply.

"What do you mean, nothing? Who's Negrín?"

"A client who owes me money. Better to forget it."

"That's what I'm saying, Dad. Sometimes losing a deal is gaining in health."

"That's right, sweetheart. Better to forget."

In that magazine for fools, Don Jordi thought, was the most important date of his life. But other questions remained. How could a worker, rather poor like his father, have known about the secret movements of the president of the Republic of Spain, even if it was a dying republic?

"*The poet died far from home...*" he murmured.

"*...Covered by the dust of a neighboring country*", continued Lucía. "I love Serrat... *As he walked away, they saw him cry, traveler, there is no path, the path is made by walking...*"

Hey, Dad, did you know the lyrics refer to Antonio Machado?

"Yes, of course. I'm not as educated as you, but I'm still Spanish."

"*Spain, white shirt of my hope…*"

Jacksonville, 2013

The Letters of Mijail Polzin

February 15, 2001 Alejandro Polzin left Buenos Aires on an American Airlines flight. The decision bore Alejandro's trademark. He didn't say goodbye to anyone. He didn't prepare anyone to replace him; perhaps the opposite. A few hours before taking a taxi to Ezeiza Airport, during an unusual visit to La Boca, he calmly threw his two cell phones into the Riachuelo and dropped his resignation letter into a mailbox.

Those who knew him understood that he had left for good. When a man like Alejandro breaks something, his colleagues said, he breaks it without leaving room for repairs. Any rectification or backtracking offends them, and since they don't know how to express their emotions as well as they express their ideas, they need to shatter an ancient Chinese vase to make clear the high value of such an object. Everyone imagined him somber and resolute, though not angry. Ernesto Iturria, the project director, guessed that at some point Alejandro must have considered the architects and investors, imagined them running around desperately in the futile task of finding a replacement, and must have smiled. Paula, the boss's secretary, who had discreetly endured his indifference, was more precise and convincing: the engineer had ruined his career and his life over an ungrateful love. She didn't mention a name, but in the office, everyone knew who she was referring to.

Beatrice didn't find out until, alarmed by the impossibility of reaching him by phone, she went to look for him at the apartment on Corrientes Street and a neighbor gave her the news. The engineer had left on a trip with two suitcases that suggested he would be away for some time. She wrote to him once, but he didn't respond.

Almost ten years later, Alejandro returned incognito and visited the streets he frequented during happier days. One morning, he saw the open windows of the fifth-floor apartment facing Las Heras Park, which he had rented with Beatrice for a year. "The best year of my life," he remembered admitting once. And Beatrice, with a half-smile, her lips slightly parted, her eyes closed, and her breasts relaxed, had asked him why he said "the best year" and not "the happiest year." Alejandro didn't understand. Apparently, neither did Beatrice. She couldn't explain the difference. So, what was the point of the distinction?

Strangely, he remembered the scent of the perfume she used, but not the name or the apartment number. Strangely, because a man like Alejandro always remembers numbers better, except for anniversaries. Scents are women's things.

Beatrice had become an obsession. He thought of her whenever he wasn't with her.

In the afternoon, he went to Palermo. He had gotten her address thanks to the indiscretion of an old acquaintance. He saw her step out of a silver car with a blond-haired child. He guessed the child was about three years old.

When he visited his father in Once, neither of them brought up Beatrice. Only when the old man was about to ask him the reasons for his disappearance did Alejandro steer the conversation elsewhere. He mentioned that he had been in Moscow.

"In Moscow?"

"Yes."

"In Moscow…" the old man repeated.

Over the years, his face had grown dull. The lines that defined it had become blurred, imprecise, almost expressionless. The old man, Alejandro thought in a split second, was increasingly incapable of crying or laughing. Those characteristics that had once set them so apart had faded. Over the years, his father had become more like him and his grandfather.

"Yes, in Russia…"

On the other hand, they had always shared certain other peculiarities, family traits. His father had as much difficulty talking about certain topics as he did. It was easier for him to discuss politics or soccer than his brothers, whom he hadn't visited since 1976, or the cataracts that had diminished his vision. Perhaps that's why he had specialized in more complex and entirely impersonal discussions.

"When?" he finally asked.

"About a year ago, more or less."

"You didn't tell me," said his father.

The comment was unnecessary. Like everything, thought Alejandro.

"I brought you a cap that belonged to a soldier from the Second World War. I bought it at a street fair, though it's probably fake, like everything in Russia these days. Even capitalism is fake there. The practices for getting rich are more like those in Sicily than in Wall Street."

The old man shook his head. He was about to ask about the difference between Sicily and Wall Street but quickly realized it was pointless. They'd end up in another argument.

"That's good. But you should have written sooner," he said; "I know of places I would have liked you to visit, since I never could."

Another unnecessary remark. The old man knew Alejandro wasn't one to comment on or announce his plans.

"What did you think?"

"Nothing. I felt nothing. To me, they were like strangers."

The faces and a few names had reminded him of his uncles, of Anastasia's daughters, of Grandfather Mijail. The noses made for the cold, the drooping eyelids, but above all the way they looked, both sad and happy, as if they had just woken up from a nap they never actually slept.

"Of course," his father observed. "We stopped belonging to that culture a long time ago. We're strangers. We're gauchos who drink mate in a city where you can hardly see the trees and the snow never bothers us. No one would ever know your grandparents were Russian if it weren't for the last name. You never had anything to do with Russians. You didn't even learn a single word of Russian."

"I learned a few last year. Just enough to get by."

"Like any tourist."

"Yes. You didn't learn Russian either."

"A few words, unavoidable ones. Some very funny insults. You know why."

He had told him many times, enough times to suspect it wasn't true or perhaps just a minor truth that served to hide something more serious. Grandfather had made sure his sons were Argentine or anything else; just not Russian. He never spoke to them in that language. For his wife, Grandmother Clara, and for his children, Cyrillic was just an incomprehensible web of symbols. Incomprehensible and useless.

"*Inconvenient*. That's the word," Alejandro corrected."

"Yes, yes, of course. It was also inconvenient…"

Still, Grandfather could never speak Spanish without a foreign accent. And he couldn't help getting angry when the neighborhood kids shouted "Russian" at him. "How old are you, boy?" Grandfather Mijail would ask. "Eight," the child would reply. "Then I'm more Argentine than you. I've lived in this country for ten years."

His father's smile at the end of the anecdote was always the same, too.

Grandfather also couldn't help getting angry in Russian. He cursed in Russian, insulted in Russian. He would never know if he also reserved his true language for when he made love or for asking for help or forgiveness when he froze to death in his car one night, stranded on the side of Route 51, on the way to the Bahía Blanca estate. In the back seat, they found a coat that could have saved him, but inexplicably the old man hadn't used it.

Once again, Alejandro reproached his father for Grandfather not having had the intelligence or the slightest interest in leaving him the greatest asset he could have now, that language so few speak in Argentina. Since living in the United States, he had understood the economic importance of culture and, above all, of a language like Russian. This inexplicable ignorance had kept him below other bilingual employees in the company who were often sent abroad.

"It was different back then," the old man said. "We were poor workers in a time when not knowing how to speak a language like Russian was more important than speaking it. The old man didn't want his sons to be persecuted or discriminated against for it."

This explanation had never convinced him. Now he simply didn't even consider it a good excuse. Another truth that crumbled on its own, like the Berlin Wall, without need and without the desire to give it a little push to see if it would hold. He remembered his childhood, always admiring everything Grandfather Mijail represented, like an impeccable patriarch. A practical man, more intelligent than reasonable, capable of solving everyone else's problems and with a clear idea of how to save Argentina from the progressive decline that had set in after the war.

But over time, Grandfather Mijail had shrunk. While listening to his father repeat the same explanations, Grandfather had already been reduced to the handful of dust that was his body in an urn in Chacarita.

Grandfather had denied him the best inheritance he could have left: a piece of the heart of Russia. On the contrary, he had made sure it wouldn't happen. Which is why his visit to Russia was like that of any stupid tourist, looking for photographs in a cardboard set. His insensitivity to the language, the food, and the history of Russia had turned into resentment toward Grandfather.

Like every brilliant grandfather, Grandfather Mijail had made a fortune from nothing and had died among the ruins of a glorious past that barely survived through anecdotes. Grandfather had left them nothing, apart from a handful of memories his father kept in the safe. A useless but curious watch, coins with promises of unfulfilled value, keys, keychains, pieces of some unrecognizable artifact. And a cardboard box with letters written in Russian.

Alejandro had never forgotten those letters, but he had also never shown any interest in them. That day, he realized he had almost missed the only chance to uncover his grandfather's secrets. The most important things are almost always irreversible and are decided in an instant before our eyes, without us even noticing. Almost always, it's our own fault, like when we invest everything in rising stocks that are about to collapse. Even when we read the cause of the future collapse in the headline of the *Wall Street Journal*," inflation in China, a French CEO caught in the act of attempted rape—, we fail to recognize them as a future cause, and sometimes we even take pleasure in others' misfortune, unaware that it's our own ruin.

Without hesitation, he asked his father for the letters, promising to return them soon. His father handed them over, saying they were his, with the only condition that he take care of them as he had for fifty years.

Alejandro didn't know what to do with the rest of his days in Buenos Aires. Like any tourist, he went to Caminito and San Telmo. He dropped a few dollars into the hat of a bandoneon player, who thanked him with *Adiós Nonino*. That night, he dined alone at Happening. He strolled through Plaza de Mayo. He declined a girl's invitation to continue the conversation at her apartment and later regretted it when he arrived at the Once hotel.

The day before returning to New York, he passed through Palermo. He parked the car not far from Beatrice's apartment. He confirmed that with age, he had lost his capacity for wonder. When he was young, he could spend hours entranced, gazing at the city's skyline, the lights that began to flicker on at dusk. Over time, he had learned to survive, to solve problems. He had become a practical man, like his grandfather. Maybe that's why, he thought, few things moved him anymore. Russia had been a bad experience. Now, not even the nostalgia for Buenos Aires had managed to bother him after ten years. Nothing.

He got out of the car, absorbed in these thoughts, and didn't notice that Beatrice was watching him. Though she wore dark glasses, she must have recognized him, perhaps not without some doubt. When he realized, he stopped, and she quickened her pace until she disappeared into the building's lobby.

Alejandro walked in the opposite direction. He circled the block, pretended to enter a bar, and then left again.

When he thought Beatrice would have gone upstairs, he headed toward the building. The city had suddenly darkened, and the streetlights hadn't yet come on.

When he finally reached the building's entrance, he saw her face expressionless but with eyes that revealed she had been crying. It wasn't just an impression; Alejandro knew those eyes. They had changed somewhat, but they were the same eyes that cried over any little thing and then forced her to wear dark glasses for the rest of the day.

Beatrice hurriedly inserted the key and entered without looking back. He remembered those eyes that had once said, "It was my cousin, one of my best friends." And he had corrected her: "Good friends don't hug like that." And she had replied, "Grandpa died."

After a moment, Alejandro searched for her name on the intercom panel. None of them revealed anything. He tried in vain to remember and connect surnames.

He saw two older women enter, a young woman who smiled at him, three boys with books laughing loudly at a joke, one who rang a buzzer and someone opened the door with an insult. He saw a man his age, impeccably dressed and with an expressionless gaze. Then an elderly woman complaining about her poor eyesight as she struggled to fit the key into the lock. Finally, the doorman, who had seen him hesitating, came out and asked if he was looking for someone.

The first Saturday in Manhattan, he went to the Russian Glinka's store. If he hadn't gone more often, it was to avoid the excessive familiarity with which the old man, who fancied himself a poet, treated him. He felt uncomfortable with peddlers like old Glinka, the Japanese woman in Chinatown, or the Turks at the Bazaar Otoyolu, who were cheerful and friendly with the sole purpose of selling their trinkets. He felt more at ease with a waitress in upper Manhattan who smiled warmly at him every time she served him at a restaurant, or a beautiful employee who said *"sweeeeet,"* while trying to sell him a shirt or a

TV. The capitalist lie seemed more sincere to him, he admitted, with a proud sideways smile. That's what he paid for without haggling, to be sold a bit of joy when he left work. And that's what they paid him for too, to show his boss and his clients that he was happy, even if he was dying.

Alejandro proceeded in the only way he could without being paralyzed by overthinking. He placed the box of letters on the little table where old Glinka did his accounts and drank vodka at dusk. He told him he needed them translated, without urgency. The task couldn't be a burden for the old man, who ran that business more to keep himself occupied than out of necessity.

But instead of the enthusiasm Alejandro had imagined, he found surprise and perplexity.

Old Glinka hesitated. He wanted to know more. He placed his hand on the little box to stop Alejandro from opening it. He asked whose letters they were, if he was sure about what he was about to do.

Alejandro also hesitated. He admitted he wasn't sure. A strong smell of vodka reminded him of his grandfather's kitchen in his final years. For a moment, his breathing quickened; he hadn't completely overcome, as he thought, the shyness of his adolescence.

He hadn't even considered that translating old, yellowed letters over eighty years old could, in some way, be a mistake. There was a reason they were eighty years old and probably just as long since they had become a tangle of symbols no one could read. There was a reason his grandfather had been so secretive. There was a reason neither he nor his father had ever thought to find out what they said.

For a little over a year, Alejandro learned to buy whiskey and *kapusta* at a store in lower Manhattan. He spent his free hours reading the latest news. He became addicted to the *Wall Street Journal* and once had the intuition that he had discovered the geometric logic of the Dow Jones. When he wasn't in *Union Square* with his *iPad*, he would stop by an Apple store and distract himself playing with the latest gadgets. There was always something new in the digital world, he thought, but in the end, it was all the same.

"Among the infinite variations of the same thing" he thought, almost amazed at what he was thinking, "like an Andy Warhol painting, nothing is different. These neat people will never know what it's like to smell a mud ranch in the Pampas, with a wood stove and kerosene lantern light."

As soon as he finished writing this in his email, he deleted it. Who could he send it to? Himself? Yes, that's what he did most of the time, emailing himself. But he deleted it.

He did things more out of obligation and less because he wanted to. That's why, he thought, he did them better each time. He didn't make mistakes. He didn't get depressed or bitter over any failure. And if any bothersome doubt visited him some night, he chased it away with a good Johnnie Walker, which was why he worked, so they'd leave him alone when he wasn't working. Some idiot living in Santiago, Chile, once told him he was becoming too Americanized. Like all idiots, he arrogated the right to moralize about other people's lives and felt superior because he had failed in all his attempts to do something with his own life.

When something went wrong, he attributed it to probabilities or a miscalculation. As they say here, to a "lack of judgment," though in Spanish that means something else. How do you say "lack of judgment" in Russian?

One day he returned to Glinka's store. If he hadn't gone before, it was because of overthinking, a small existential crisis, typical of those in their 30s or 40s. The old man had had a heart attack and was recovering in a dark corner, among bags of rice and curry, dates, and dried figs he had added to meet the growing demand from Arabs in the neighborhood.

He had taken on the moribund appearance of Grandfather Mikhail. The same straight nose, the slightly resigned lips, the eyes hidden beneath heavy eyelids, the same clear forehead faintly outlined by sparse white hair. The same lack of energy to smile. That was the grandfather he had known. He hadn't imagined—now he realized—that the real one, the grandfather who had been for most of his life, was someone else. Someone else, perhaps more energetic, perhaps as insensitive as he was in his forties, a tireless lover of women who didn't love him back in his twenties and a young poet who enjoyed the twilight lights of Moscow in his early adolescence.

Old Glinka gestured with his hand. Alejandro approached.

"*The letters,*" he said.

"I didn't bring them," Alejandro replied.

"Bring them," Glinka said, in a tone that sounded like an order without authority, almost a plea.

Alejandro didn't respond.

"I owe you a favor," the old man insisted. "Not a day has gone by without me thinking about it. I don't know how I could refuse…"

Alejandro tried to reassure him. As always, he thought, one only knows how to reassure others.

"Now it's you who must do me this favor…," the old man pressed.

Alejandro promised to bring the letters by Saturday.

"No, not Saturday. I'll be very busy on Saturday. Friday…"

On Friday, a little before six, Alejandro brought the letters. Glinka ordered his five employees to close up and leave.

The two of them sat at a small table in a corner, under a dusty yellow light.

Old Glinka opened the little cardboard box as if it were a sacred chest or an archaeological delicacy. Alejandro attributed it to age and fatigue, not to the importance of the letters. The old man flipped through them one by one, arranging them like a deck of cards. Alejandro asked if he was sorting them by date. After a distracted "no," the old man said yes. It was the dates. "More or less," he corrected himself afterward.

For two hours, old Glinka read with difficulty and translated from Russian to English, line by line, fumbling for the best words, correcting himself, sometimes groping, like a blind man, for some meaning in so many obscure expressions.

The content of the letters was somewhat disappointing. Nothing important, no secret that would shame his grandfather, no extraordinary inheritance still unclaimed. Reality is often quite boring, Glinka consoled him. Or it seems to be. Perhaps if he looked more carefully and with feeling at those distant events, those recent confessions, he would discover what only a biologist is capable of seeing in a monotonous cell.

Almost half of the letters were full of metaphors. Nine had been written by Grandfather Mikhail, serving as drafts or having been returned. Almost all were addressed to his mother, Karina, except for one that seemed to speak to a brother. Eleven letters were from his mother, all longer than the grandfather's and easier to read. They were full of motherly advice, Alejandro thought. They didn't offer anything new, apart from warnings about the benefits of good nutrition and certain instructions to guard against ear infections, which, according to his mother, were typical of the Polzins; a torment Alejandro had suffered in recent years and had attributed to the cold of New York.

The Polzin family hadn't belonged to the nobility, but neither had the grandfather been the poor man he had claimed to be before becoming a prosperous builder in Buenos Aires. He had some disagreements with the new Soviet regime, which, it was known, would eventually dominate the entire world in a few decades, but politics wasn't his strong suit, nor had he ever been interested in it. Even less in ideological debates. He said that ideas led nowhere and were all preceded by the actions of pragmatic men like him. The grandfather didn't consider this an idea. Alejandro thought his pragmatism had saved him from all the regimes of the time, though not from the dignity of fools who died for certain ideals. In this, he was very much like him and nothing like his father, who surely must have suffered with the grandfather as much as he, Alejandro, had to endure the philosophical moralizing of his father. The ideological silence that characterized the grandfather was due to this disinterest and not to the stoic guarding of a secret past that he had skillfully allowed to grow around him through misunderstandings.

In short, the grandfather's life had been quite simple. It was almost devoid of interest.

Around eleven at night, old Glinka struggled to straighten his back. He sighed wearily, and Alejandro told him they should leave it for another day. The old man agreed. Only two letters remained. The most difficult ones, he said, because of the handwriting. They agreed that Alejandro would leave them with him so he could study them better and without haste, in the light of day.

Later, he learned that one letter, dated March 25, 1928, was from a certain Aleksandra. It was full of questions about the grandfather's trip to America. Aleksandra had been his girlfriend or lover for almost a year.

Apparently, the grandfather never answered this letter. Instead—Alejandro speculated—he sketched a long prose poem. Alejandro thought that the mere form of verse would have shamed his grandfather. But he felt no shame—perhaps he foresaw that his confession would not be read in his lifetime—when he confessed that the most beautiful woman in Russia had given him the best year of his life. A woman can only give her best year once. They loved each other in the finest hotels, in the cheapest boarding houses, and even in the parks of Moscow. They loved each other madly in winter and summer. The grandfather had never forgotten her perfect face, her twenty-year-old body, her fantasies of a happy marriage, like a princess, like a fairy tale. All that absurd madness had lasted eleven and a half months, and afterward, according to the grandfather's poetic confession, there was no way to return to reality without dying. But he had decided to keep living.

"The typical romantic love of the 19th century# Alejandro commented. "Love is so perfect that the lovers or fate decide to end it... I suppose that by 1928 all that sentimentality would have already gone out of style in Russia.

Glinka smiled. He wanted to be complicit in Alejandro's critique. In fact, it was an irrefutable critique; it was true, all that had passed.

"Men do things that have no explanation—old Glinka acknowledged. "If we were more sensible, we'd be less happy but we wouldn't suffer so much."

And that description of the eyes blue as the sky, Alejandro thought, was terribly bad. Lucky the grandfather hadn't dedicated himself to poetry. He wouldn't have earned much.

"Cheesy," Alejandro declared.

The old man didn't reply. He pursed his lips as presidents do when they deliver bad news or admit to some infidelity.

"She betrayed him," Alejandro said.

"It's not clear," the old man said. "In her letter, she defends herself. They had been rumors from her brother. Apparently, your grandfather also punished him, or wanted to punish him with silence. Nowhere does it show that he answered her letter."

He searched for one.

"This one," said old Glinka, holding up one of the letters, "this is the letter where your grandfather's brother mentions the story of the girl with her boss at a restaurant... According to her, it hadn't been a private lunch but a work lunch. The other employee was in the bathroom when someone they knew (what was his name?) passed by."

"I'm sorry to have wasted your time, Mr. Glinka," said Alejandro.

The old man looked at him as if he couldn't quite make out his face in the darkness.

"What did you say?"

"I apologize for having wasted your time with these trivialities."

The old man didn't respond. He leaned on Alejandro's shoulder, walked to the counter, and sat in his usual chair.

"We'll finish tomorrow," he said. "It's very late, and these bones can't stay upright anymore."

Alejandro took the letters, except for the last one that remained untranslated, thanked old Glinka with a pat on the back, and left.

Old Glinka died on Friday night or early Saturday morning. Contradicting his doctor, he had been working until the last moment on the translation of the final letter. On the table were some scribbles in Russian and English. None of them, Alejandro thought, had anything to do with Aleksandra and Grandfather Mikhail. They were other names of men and women, other cities in Ukraine. Too many abbreviations, his wife said, impossible to know what they meant. It was as if the old man had feared someone else might understand them.

"When one is very young," old Glinka had scribbled in the margin of a translation, "one persistently seeks to be what one wants to be, almost always a copy of some famous stranger; rebellion brings one closer to something different from what one will become with time: a timid variation, more successful or more frustrated, of one's parents, grandparents, all those ancestors one has never known and therefore cannot suspect how much one resembles them. Freedom is always there, but one almost never achieves awareness and exercise of it, at least not much beyond its illusory substitutes."

In truth, even the old man himself hadn't understood them. He had been making the effort to understand himself and probably hadn't had enough time.

Alejandro apologized and left the old store. He knew he was fleeing from something that now surrounded the widow. The widow would have to carry all that sadness for the next few hours, for the years to come.

It's not my business, Alejandro thought. Soon he would pass by that street and see a new store, renovated, brighter. Maybe an Apple or Microsoft store. It would be good for the block, which was a bit dull.

He walked to *South Cove Plaza*. It was getting dark. At that hour, almost all the benches facing the river were empty. He sat on one, near a girl who seemed to be holding back laughter. She was reading something on her phone, and black leather boots accentuated the elegance of her long, young legs. A moment later, he noticed the girl was crying inconsolably.

He was about to approach her to offer help. But he realized how ridiculous the scene would be and left in time. He knew that if he didn't rest well on Sundays, he couldn't perform during the week. And that put him in a very bad mood.

Jacksonville, 2014

A new kind of cold

Guadalupe had never experienced a cold like the one in Philadelphia. At the bus stop, she huddled, trying to cover her son's little body with her own. But the shelter was barely like a transparent eggshell, and the wind crept underneath and swirled above. The bus hadn't come yet and probably wouldn't. Either Guadalupe didn't know that it never came after six, or she thought it had broken down on the way. She hadn't imagined it would be dark by then; otherwise, she would have brought the fur coat José had given her on her last birthday in Arizona.

When it was almost dark, a car passed by and stopped. A voice from inside called her name, but Guadalupe didn't answer. They shouted again for her to get in the car, but Guadalupe didn't answer. So the car screeched its tires on the asphalt and sped away.

"Don't be scared, baby," Guadalupe said softly. "don't startle, my little one."

The child fell back asleep.

The mother's purple fingers stroked the child's blond hair.

"Blondie," José had said, "how is it possible that the kid is blond when there are no blondes in the family?

Don't be stupid, Nacho had told him, all kids are born with eyes that light. You're just a kid without children who doesn't know anything about that, José had shouted. Don't you dare try to educate me. Don't be crazy, José, just because you're a father doesn't make you wiser. They say you're not a pianist just because you have a piano. That remains to be seen, so shut up and finish that dough or the boss will fire us both. That's how you're going to repay me for getting you the job."

As if these newcomers are going to educate me. Latino parents and a son as blond as a Yankee. And even if it's true that Machito's hair and eyes got darker over time, he's still blond. His hair is like Sofía's, that little Argentine girl who drove us crazy at Taco Bell. Fine, blond hair. What does Machito have of the Reyes? Nothing. Lupe defends herself by saying one of her grandmothers was blond. But the old woman died before Lupe realized she had a blond, blue-eyed grandmother. What a coincidence, right? If it's not a lie from Lupe, it's a lie from her mother, famous in San Salvador for making things up. Maybe the blond Indian existed, but she just had to ruin my life. I had to ask Chapo, who knows computers, to retouch some photos of Machito, make them darker or something, fix them to send to the family. Let's see if they leave me alone. They already have enough with the money I send them, I don't know what else they want.

José Reyes turned right and headed back to the stop where Guadalupe was.

"The fool doesn't know there are no buses at this hour."

But before arriving, he knew Guadalupe wouldn't agree to get in the car. He stopped, turned off the radio, thought for a moment, and finally decided not to go there. He couldn't handle another rejection from Lupe. Let's see if she learns not to play hard to get.

He took the highway to Camden. As he crossed the New Jersey bridge, it began to snow. During the two years they were in Arizona, Guadalupe had hoped it would snow. She had never seen snow in her life. In Arizona, there's no snow, Guadalupe, that's why it's called Arizona and not Nevada. But Guadalupe had seen postcards of the Grand Canyon in winter. That's far from here, Guadalupe, maybe we can go next year. We couldn't go because there was never time, her scrubbing the floors at the Radisson and me making tacos and pizza. And when I lost my job in a raid, we fled to the north. On the Greyhound, she told me she was going to see the snow. And she was right, we couldn't escape that.

José turned the windshield wipers to full speed. Snow at sixty miles per hour is like a trip to the stars in one of those ridiculous movies where the stars pass by the side of the ship. More like entering a tube, or swimming through a school of fish in the Caribbean.

But colder, much colder, thought José. Everything is colder here. Cold like the cold blondes of the north.

Ewing, 2010

The second death of
Jordi Caballero

His father died again when Jordi turned thirty-five. He was
that age when he last saw him in Barcelona, that Thursday,
February 9, 1939.

Until then, he could look in the mirror and see his father's face, the gaze anxious for a sudden hope or weary
from a new failure. All his intimacies had also been his father's. Every time his eyes followed the backside of a
woman passing by the window of a bar where he read the
newspaper next to a steaming coffee, it was his father's gesture in the Barcelona of the thirties or the Madrid of the
twenties. At least that's what he believed. He believed that
one more or less repeats the dreams and frustrations of
their ancestors in different settings. Then, he would close
his eyes and see the grandfather he never knew, Grandfather Caballero (his name was Jordi, just like him, just like
his father, because of that old habit people had of not being content with just passing down the surname to their
children, burdened or haunted by a useless longing for
eternity) climbing a stone path beside the mountain,
shielding himself from the snow, dragging a cart with a
skinny mule, trying to start an old Ford in Oviedo with his

son watching anxiously from inside the broken-down car. And he saw his father discovering the world in Madrid, at a lonely little table in the corner of a workers' bar, with an old pen, and it was himself in the bar on Canelones and Ciudadela with a cell phone in his hand.

He couldn't imagine in detail any of those other people who came before his grandfather, who miraculously saved their lives so that, without intending to, he, Jordi (Jordi the third, Jordi the fourth), would be there looking at the little Renoir painting. But ultimately, all those were details that don't change what really matters in the human experience: love, jealousy, the pain of injustice and moral violence, the insult, the threat from a stranger or an unhinged neighbor, the death of a grandfather, of an uncle, the guilt of having done the right thing or of having made an irreparable mistake. All of that is reality. Or rather, the deepest reality of reality. The rest are just settings. As if in every era, in every generation, in every century, the same play were staged. Romeo and Juliet in Verona. Romeo and Juliet in Paris during World War II. Romeo and Juliet in John Lennon's New York or in Tinelli's Buenos Aires. Romeo and Juliet walking the dusty streets of a Chinese village. Romeo and Juliet dying on the Gaza border.

Until Don Jordi turned thirty-five, all those images of that distant, understanding, and sometimes absent father had taken shape. The mustache of his father hiding imperfect teeth. His kind words that embraced that child who was Don Jordi, like his own when he tried to comfort and, above all, protect with advice his little girl with her thin arms, more to prevent other pains in the woman he imagined Lucía would become than to ease her fears and frustrations.

What he lacked, however (Don Jordi told himself, resorting to those secret forms of self-flagellation that a person haunted by a hidden sense of guilt always finds), was all the idealism of his father. That political idealism, republican by circumstance, which he had long looked upon with disdain and only as he approached thirty-five could feel, at least in part, when in a fit of romantic madness he gifted a small farm in San José to the family he had hired to care for the fruit trees. Every so often he would stop by, and the couple's five children would come out to greet him as if he were the founding father of a micro-republic. The father, whom the neighbors called the Negro Silva, had hung a sign at the entrance that read "Caballero Farm."

Once again, he got involved in an unnecessary fraud back in the seventies, during the dictatorship. He had managed to evade thirty percent of that year's taxes. A move that was unworthy of Don Jordi, he told himself, not because it was dishonest—if not paying taxes is even dishonest—but because of how rudimentary the maneuver was. Someone noticed and filed a complaint. For a few weeks, he felt the vertigo of being pursued. He could have gotten involved with one of the factions, with some group of dissidents in exile, with the artists in Libertad prison who painted abstract doves and weeping butterflies, or with one of those sects or lodges the military would occasionally set up to feel important. He could have tried something more elegant than a crude evasion, he thought when the storm passed, which cost him a considerable sum to avoid prison and keep his name out of the newspapers. At least it would have been more honorable.

But he lacked some of the ingredients that made his father who he was, he thought. He lacked courage. He lacked that stupid idealism that made and unmade his father and his mother. At least that's what he wanted to think, since the possibility that his father might have actually been much more like him than he could imagine terrified him. He didn't want to tarnish certain memories. It would have been like demolishing the central pillars of his existence. Perhaps he preferred not to know the full truth. Or maybe he didn't have enough wisdom to understand that even heroes defecate and participate, through some actions, in the marketplace of human miseries.

But when he turned thirty-five, he realized he could no longer keep discovering his father in his own fears, in his joys, in his obsessions, in his tics, in his unjustified sadnesses, in one too many drinks. From then on, he had to walk alone. When he reached the age his father was when he disappeared, when he died or was killed, he knew that everything new he could feel and experience in this life had been foreign to that other Jordi Caballero: the depressions of the forties; the less frequent erections; the worries of raising a teenager; the sometimes arrogant pragmatism; the absolute lack of fear of public speaking; the inability to be moved by the scent of lavender or the presence of the naked sea; the increasing scarcity of beautiful women who deigned to look him in the eye; the growing hatred of the younger ones who couldn't find paths to reach where he stood, like a dictator usurping a public and private space for an excessively prolonged time; the suspicion that people were beginning to view his death with growing indifference; the awareness of being on a boat that was moving away from the shore, moving away from the world of the young who were beginning to occupy the cities and rewrite the history of themselves and their elders.

He knew that none of those inner landscapes had been part of his father's world, who had died so young. All of that was now his world, and he had to discover it alone. From the age of thirty-five onward, he had to start living alone. His father had died for the second time and, even so, he knew that this was not a definitive death either.

Jacksonville, 2011

The raft

La blasa was shaped like a fish. It was, in reality, a large piece of some other metallic apparatus. Judging by some details, it must have been part of a larger vessel, one of those futuristic ships that once sailed the skies and outer space. The future had ended in 1979. The ship had something of the Apollo 13 and the *shuttles* like the Discovery or the Atlantis that came a little later.

Perhaps it had been a combat plane or a submarine in distress that had surfaced, like a ship sinking in reverse. It still retained part of the engines or the nearly useless fuselage; the only purpose of all that metal down there was to somewhat stabilize the drifting remains and prolong their agony on the surface and, above all, to keep the sole passenger occupied, who had always lived obsessed with the enigma of those twisted pieces of metal.

But the ship didn't stay afloat on its own. Its sole passenger and crew member spent all day ensuring it didn't abandon the surface of the sea and head to port. For that, every day he had to remove the water that accumulated in its belly. That's how it had been for as long as he could remember. For more than thirty weeks, he managed to keep that mass of steel and aluminum afloat. On rainy days, he collected fresh water, and on stormy days, the task of reducing the water in the hold was delayed, sometimes beyond the tolerable limits according to his calculations.

Not despite his solitude but because of it, there were few days when the man could rest. There was always something urgent to do on la blasa. The few and almost exceptional hours of rest he dedicated to lying under the green tarp. Inexplicably, he was drawn to the stains on the tarp that came to life under the different suns and moons that penetrated it. Sometimes they resembled sea monsters. Other times they were like gods descending austerely from the sky or rising sensually from the waters. He had in mind the image of a woman he didn't know but who felt familiar to him. Of all the images, it was the one that appeared most often in the reflections on the green tarp, especially when exhaustion overtook him at dusk and he lay sprawled out, drunk on sweat and satisfaction after having reduced the water in the hold to a minimum in a fit of rage and weariness.

But he didn't give in to simple complacency. His hours of rest were few and strictly limited by his responsible impatience. He knew that if an emergency found him exhausted, it could mean the end of his days. His mind had to be clear and alert; his muscles always ready to spring into action and endure long hours of tension, going up and down the stairs to reduce the water, holding the ropes so the wind wouldn't carry away the sail and the mast, making sure no piece of metal could slip off the ship. In his life, he had thrown himself into the sea many times to rescue insignificant pieces of wood, plastic boxes, bottles, and even a chair, but he knew that a piece of metal that fell into the water, whether a tool or a simple nut, would sink like a lightning bolt into the darkest abyss.

On rare occasions, he allowed himself the luxury of looking at the magazines on la blasa. There weren't many, but he took care of them because they were sacred. Though they were written in some incomprehensible language he had never given up trying to understand (he knew that symbols are like clouds and stars; those who can read them can know the present and predict the future), he could still understand their images. A very beautiful woman, with fish-colored hair and dressed in coral red, dominated the main magazine, from the cover to the centerfold. She was almost naked, and he adored her like the sun, which is why he only allowed himself to admire her on full moon nights, since it was on a moonlit night that he had discovered her and on a moonlit night that he had felt his entire body tremble at her presence. When he saw the photos inside, he knew it was her, the same woman in different poses, with different moods. Along with other women who surrounded her, they waited in some place shaped like a giant ship on an infinite deck, surrounded by green clouds without a sea.

In all the magazines, there were women and men like him, almost always smiling, lying on the sand of a beach (that place where the world ends and Paradise begins) or walking down a huge hallway surrounded by very tall buildings. There was one that particularly impressed him because it reminded him of dreams he had had long before discovering the magazines. It was the image of a city with many very tall buildings seen from the sea. He always imagined that one morning he would wake up and, looking toward the horizon, would see the city rising from the calm waters of the West.

On sunny days, the man would raise the makeshift sail and steer the ship toward the setting sun. He wasn't sure why or when he had chosen that direction. He reflected on this first decision for months and at some point concluded that it was the right one. First, because that was the direction the sun took every day. Second, because it was more practical to maintain the course of a lost ship to avoid a wandering or circular route that would dangerously prolong the shipwreck. Sooner or later, he had to reach somewhere, or the world was an infinite ocean, without respite.

However, it took him a long time to learn to navigate using the stars. The movement of the night stars was much more complex than the simple movement of the sun, and, on the other hand, he had taken the habit of sleeping at night, not during the day, which prevented him from gaining any knowledge about the cosmic order of the things high above. For this reason, he knew that perhaps his navigation hadn't always maintained the same direction.

Maybe at night he veered toward some other cardinal point. Maybe he retraced the path he had taken during the day. Only the smiling woman could tell him one day.

Over time, he dismissed this second possibility. Indeed, he had sailed *toward some part* of the universe. During the day, the sun took a different path, more slanted and colder, as if it had aged. As a logical consequence, the waters had grown colder and were no longer as transparent as they had been at the beginning, as he remembered, though with a certain sweet vagueness, perhaps attributable to nostalgia.

In the last two weeks especially, the waters had shown a troubling change. They had become colder, dirtier, sadder, and sometimes more interesting. Almost daily, he spotted some plastic object on the horizon, as if it had belonged to some other blasa like his own. He couldn't imagine another sailor throwing pieces of their ship overboard, because he knew how valuable these materials were—like teeth, once lost, they could not be recovered, and with each loss, they drew closer to the fate of the fish that end up in their own bellies or in the bellies of other fish. Every day he discovered some new evidence of the death of a fellow sailor, and he would dive into the water to retrieve it.

The new debris always had some use. Sometimes it would meet a need that had gone unmet for days, like a piece of wood that replaced a small pillar holding up the green tarp under which he napped and communed with the gods. Other times, it would rest in the semi-flooded hold, waiting for some purpose.

Another significant change that followed the increase in debris was the birds. White birds with black beaks that flew much higher than the bright fish of the early days. Those fish had been harmless, like the dolphins and the transparent waters, but these flying creatures seemed almost as threatening as the sharks that followed him day and night, waiting for the final shipwreck.

He knew there was no salvation left. If he sank, the sharks would tear his body to pieces; if he died on the ship, the black-beaked birds would do the same under the sun before the blasa sank.

For days this thought haunted him as he adjusted the sail to speed up his journey. Incredibly, in the last week he had managed to double his speed thanks to the new position he had given the sail.

One morning, the miracle happened. The city was there. Upon waking, as he did every morning, he looked to the West and saw it, between the cloudy sky and the shimmering sea. He rejoiced. He almost raised his arms in triumph. But his heart began to beat violently. Not even in the worst storms had he experienced such uncontrollable pounding.

He managed to calm himself, though the excitement of the discovery lingered in the blinking of his eyes and the useless movements of his hands. He reflected for a long time on the discovery until he decided to trust his survival instinct. He had realized just in time the terrible mistake he had made and upheld his entire life.

Then, just in time, he turned and set course for the warmer region, where the fish fly and the water is transparent. He headed toward where he had been born, forty weeks earlier, long after the woman with fish-colored hair had smiled to show him the true path he was only now finding.

Jacksonville, 2011

Stories of an Essayist

The Word

With growing nervousness he made triangular shapes by folding the little paper that said 22-A. He tried to think about the advantages of the A or the K over the intermediate letters. He was sure he would say the word as soon as he faced the woman at door H.

This absurd certainty had frightened him so much that, without looking anywhere, he took a step and left the line. He feigned discomfort. He took his suitcase and headed to the bathroom. He made several suspicious movements: he took a hallway full of people going in the opposite direction; he had to struggle with ten or twenty people who didn't notice someone was going against the flow. Everyone smelled of perfume, of cleanliness. The men wore black and blue suits. Even the homophobes wore pink socks and ties, because it was fashionable. Sweet perfumes predominated. One even smelled like watermelon, but without the stickiness that comes from the sugar of dried watermelon on the hand. At least five women wore real jewelry, mostly white gold. They all looked alike. They must all have been beautiful, according to the enormous beauty ads in the duty-free shop windows. Full lips of a mouth that could open and swallow a person. Giant eyes with wrinkle-free eyelids.

Although he had been born there, although he had lived there for forty years, 22-A felt like a foreigner, or something caught his attention. He was disturbed by offending the strict routine; lately he hadn't fulfilled the usual Sunday services; a recent experience in the mountains—he had been disconnected for a week, cut off by a weather accident from all the indices he loved most—had kept him under a mild but suspicious fever. His new state revealed itself in enigmatic phrases, perhaps thoughts. "One day for God," he said to a friend from the stock exchange, "six days for Money."

He took another hallway just to save himself from the current that dragged him in a compromising effort. Although he didn't know where the row of bathrooms he had used half an hour earlier was, he walked with feigned confidence. After several changes of direction that must have been picked up by the hidden cameras in the dark Christmas spheres, he found a restroom.

He entered a stall, dragging his suitcase cart, and forced himself to urinate. But he had nothing to do and feared that someone might be watching him through the air vent. A black hole revealed no glass eye. Nor its absence either.

The obscene dialogues of the sixties, which had been erased for years by the rigorous moral hygiene in place, were beginning to return in a more dignified form. In impeccable red printed letters, the company *W* wanted to remind the happy urinator that the world was in danger and needed his cooperation. Across the way, on the door, another sign warned the current defecator of the deceptions of all forms of relief and the need for permanent maximum alertness.

He tucked himself away modestly and left, absurdly nervous. What would he say if someone stopped and interrogated him? Why was he nervous? If he had nothing to hide, he wouldn't have any reason for that pallor on his face, for that revealing sweat on his hands.

While washing his hands, he saw it. This time, yes, there was a small camera. Or it pretended to be a camera, it didn't matter. Like those half-spheres hanging in big stores. Out of ten, maybe one has a camera that watches. What matters isn't whether it exists or not, but that no one can say for sure if it exists or not. A kind of agnosticism of the other's gaze was the best restraint for the basest instincts. Surveillance that no one could accuse of violating privacy, because all those were public places, including the bathroom area where people wash their hands. The cameras (or the suspicion of cameras) were there for the safety of the people themselves. In fact, no one was against this system; quite the opposite. One would have to imagine how terrible it would be if those checkpoints didn't exist. Those who occasionally dared to imagine it were horrified or wrote voluminous novels that sold like hotcakes.

For some reason, 22A understood that going to the bathroom and not being able to urinate couldn't be anything extraordinary. Less suspicious. This thought calmed him. Touching his stomach, then his head, trying to think what might have upset him, he left again, heading toward door H.

"The monster must die. What do you think?"

"Which monster?"

"Which one? Beardy."

"Oh, right, Beardy, the monster…"

"Do you doubt he's a monster?"

"Me? No, I don't doubt it. He's a monster."

"Then why do you ask *which* monster? Were you thinking of Oldbeard?"

"Well, no. Not exactly."

"What other monster could deserve to be judged in a court like the one that judged Beardy? Can you explain it to the audience of *Your News Show*?"

"Well, I don't know…"

"But you doubt."

"Yes, of course, I doubt. I firmly doubt."

"Incredible. Who are you thinking of?"

"I can't say."

"What do you mean you can't? Don't we live in a free world?"

"Yes, Sir. We live in a free world."

"Then say what you're thinking."

"I can't."

"Aren't you free to say that Beardy and Oldbeard are two monsters?"

"Yes, sir, I'm free to say it and repeat it."

"Then?"

"Am I free to say everything I think?"

"Of course. Why do you doubt it?"

"Anything I say could be used against me. It's better to be a good person."

"Of course, freedom and licentiousness aren't the same."

"Yes, Sir."

"Are you going to tell me what you were thinking?"

"Yes, sir."

"Were you thinking that thank God dictators are judged by justice?"

"Yes, sir. I've always thought that all dictators should be judged. It saddens me a little that some always escape."

"Excellent. The problem is that we don't live in a perfect world. But your words are very brave. Of course, such an act of rebellion wouldn't have been possible under a monstrous dictatorship like Beardy's or Oldbeard's."

"Yes, sir."

"Do you realize you can say it freely?"

"Yes, sir."

"Is anyone torturing you to say what you don't want to say?"

"No, sir."

"Do you understand, then, the value of freedom?"

"Yes, sir."

"Excellent. We're going back to the studio and continuing with *Your News Show*, where You are the main star. Can you hear me, Rene? Hello, can you hear me?"

But he didn't join the line he was waiting in to enter. He wanted to know if he was sure of himself. For a moment he felt better; the symptoms of panic were gone. But he still hadn't reached the certainty that, even if forced, he wouldn't utter the word. He knew that fractions of a second were enough to say it. Fractions that had been fatal for many people who, unaware of the danger, unaware of the consequences of their actions, had dared to use it in jest. He knew of the case of a foreign senator who had entered a store to buy a pen. When he passed through the checkout, the clerk asked him what it was. Why the hell did she ask that? Didn't she know that a pen is usually used for writing? Even if the pen had other functions, for example, sexual or for serving bread at breakfast, what did it matter to her what he wanted that tiny object for, sold in her own store? That is, in the store of someone she didn't know but for whom she worked day after day under those lights that didn't allow her to know if it was day or night, like in industrialized chicken coops where the good layers never see the variable light of the sun.

A pen, miss. That's what the senator should have answered. But no, the fool said the word, as if irony were recognized by the law. How stupid; irony is only recognized by intelligence. If that were *that*, the senator wouldn't have said it. He said it because that wasn't *that*, and saying it was supposed to be funny, like when the surrealists put a pipe in a museum and titled it *This is Not a Pipe*.

The senator was lucky because he was a senator. His country paid a fortune, and he was released after several days in jail. A poor devil, who knows what. A poor devil has to be very careful not to say the bad word and, moreover, not to seem like he's about to say it.

As soon as he reached this point, he realized that saying it was a matter of a slight distraction. A slight betrayal, the kind that a sick man or woman often commits against their own physical integrity, throwing themselves off a balcony for no reason or planting a kiss on the most puritanical woman on the continent, who at the same time is the boss on whom the job and life of a poor devil, a sick devil, depend.

He stood up almost rebelliously. He stood up without thinking. Suddenly he found himself standing, surrounded by people who, without stopping their hurried pace, looked at him as if he were crazy. He was starting to look suspicious, now not just to himself but to everyone else. He realized that far from helping him, the delay and the meditation were doing him harm. In bad, in terrible condition, he would reach the woman at door H. He would face the least attractive of all the officials and say the word. The more he thought about it, the more likely it became. Hadn't he been thinking about going to door H when suddenly he found himself standing, in one leap, next to his gray suitcase and the other people watching him pass by?

Suddenly, without remembering the previous steps, he found himself in front of the woman at door H, who asked him:

"Anything to declare?"

To which he responded with a silence that suspiciously began to stretch.

The woman at door H looked at him and then at the guard. The guard approached, pulling a transmitter from his belt. Two more appeared immediately.

The woman repeated the previous question.

"Anything to declare?"

"*Peace*," he said.

The guards grabbed him by the arms. He felt hydraulic pliers cutting through his muscles and finally breaking his bones.

"Peace!" he shouted this time. "A little *Peace*, yes, that's it, *Peace*! *Peace*, damn it! *Peace*, you son of a bitch!"

The guards immobilized him with a high-amperage electric shock.

He was accused in court of threatening public safety and later convicted for having concealed the word in time with the word Peace, which is also dangerous in these special times. The defense appealed the ruling citing psychiatric disturbances resulting from his recent traumatic experience in the mountains.

Atlanta, 2007

The Navel of the World, 2055

Suddenly, he suspected what everyone comes to understand, sooner or later: that he was the only living man in a world occupied by ghosts, that communication was impossible and not even desirable, that pity was as futile as hatred, that a tolerant weariness, a participation divided between respect and sensuality, were the only things that could be demanded and were worth giving.

Juan Carlos Onetti, *The Shipyard*, 1961.

At the hour when the day has not yet lost the meager warmth of the last days of summer, when people finally finish leaving their offices and the traffic jams on the outskirts of Manhattan begin to slowly dissolve, at that hour when the downtown shops close their doors and lower their steel shutters, even the pet stores, cautiously and noisily anticipating the early darkness of winter sunsets that have not yet arrived, a light and unhurried man walks south, hidden behind a white beard, almost yellow from a mysterious effect of the sunset, his gaze fixed on his next two steps, perhaps pensive or simply tired, with a gray cloth bag on his back that hints at the now cold and timid body of a saxophone. Then he stops. He ceases to murmur long and indecipherable thoughts, thoughts that drag along unclear reflections on the effects of the sunset on the melancholic mood of someone narrating their own life to themselves, and enters an old Midtown building, renovated and extremely pristine inside, carpeted against indiscreet footsteps, strategically lit so that its rooms and hallways reveal the feet and bodies entering and exiting, vaguely concealing the faces that accompany them. A pleasant scent of fruity candles fills each space, while various screens inform the customer about the services available that night.

The man with the white beard, now blue, approaches one of the machines and reads carefully. With a finger, also blue, he selects an option on the screen, and the machine issues him a ticket that says F. And, without meaning to or without thinking, like a tired man sinking distractedly into a deep sleep, he continues to reflect on the things that surround him and seep into that sudden nostalgia, like a mute and invisible hurricane entering a house and extracting from it the furniture, the pieces of doors, the paintings that hung there for years, scattering them across the city. Different hallways lead him, as in an airport, to a small door that repeats F. He enters and leaves the bundle on a small table. He sits beside it and waits. He looks: the F chamber is small and familiar, barely larger than a bathroom and devoid of the fixtures one might find in one.

One of the larger walls is made of glass and visually connects with the other twin chamber, so similar to the first that anyone might mistake the transparent glass for a mirror, if not for the detail that on the other side is not the one who is looking.

He waits for the violet light to turn on. It usually doesn't take more than three or four minutes, but one must consider that at this time of year people are more focused on their work. It won't be long; in any case, it won't be long before the light turns on and time will only begin to count from then: five minutes. And as he repeats "it won't be long," he takes the saxophone out of the bag and begins to play a few notes without much order. He suspects a malfunction in one of the buttons. The fear that the instrument might break down reminds him of the days of his youth. Until finally the light turns on and someone appears.

Someone. As expected, it's a woman. More precisely, a young woman, in a school uniform, though it's never possible to determine whether what the person is wearing actually corresponds to any of their daily activities or has been chosen for the occasion. It's almost always like that. Like the skull mask she's wearing. Many people opt for masks, because although New York is infinite, there's always the possibility that one might recognize on the street someone they might have seen in a Confessional, distorted by the blue light but sometimes recognizable by the intensity of their eyes.

[On the other hand, there are still people who feel shy about undressing, whether in a public place or in their own home. Everyone knows that at any given moment they are being filmed or listened to (by the government or by one of those private empires that have arrogated to themselves the right to decide for others), even if no one notices the presence of a camera or a hidden microphone. However, not everyone has grown accustomed to this knowledge with sufficient ease. It could happen that the official on duty recognizes the person who, in their own home, is undressing or preparing to defecate at that very moment; or that they cannot resist the temptation to publish those images on the Global Network. And while the latter is a federal crime, nothing guarantees that tomorrow or the day after, a video of a Catholic priest masturbating in some corner of New Guinea or of a poor professor's daughter exploring her virgin body in her room in São Paulo might surface. After all, crime is also a federal offense, and neither it nor all these security measures have diminished. Perhaps now it can be prevented. Not long ago, laboratory neurological studies discovered that not only do dreams produce energy waves in the brain, but so does spoken thought. From then on, it became relatively easy to realize that each word possesses a specific energy level and wave frequency, depending on the logical variations of dialects and the different emotional weight each word carries in various regions of the same country. And just as in early computing a letter or a number was the

combination of two different impulses, which later trans-
formed into words, sounds, and images, a decoding system
for spoken thought was eventually invented. As in the past,
this had important military applications, almost exclusively. From the Echelon espionage network, they moved
on to spying on the thoughts of every individual. With the
new system, nine million thoughts per second were pro-
cessed worldwide. Depending on certain thought parameters, the system selected those that might be of interest to
the Government, the company funding the Network, or
some official on duty, motivated more by chance and bore-
dom than by National Security interests. So not only were
terrorists, artists, potential philosophers, and inventors of
new commercial strategies spied on, but also famous
movie stars and everyday celebrities, creating a veritable illegal trade in erotic fantasies, mostly produced by women,
as often happened in the past with Internet images. Only
a few noticed this secret and omnipresent activity of Military Intelligence—which ultimately fulfilled the biblical
prophecy of Genesis—and denounced it ten minutes before being arrested by the Forces of Order. Those who received it through the Global Resistance Network kept it
quiet as long as they could. From this group, a minority
was not sent to asylums, because they had the rare ability—
that particular human skill of breaking all predictable
rules through sheer genius—to create new forms of en-
coded thought. As one might understand, it is not possible
to describe what kind of forms these could have been,

since no reading system could compare them to known thought parameters at the time of the programming of this God-machine. But everything has been noted by the results: many people in the world stopped thinking, at least according to the most advanced thought-reading systems. Or in fact, they were never able to think at all. And it is due to this same lack of adaptation to the progress of Global Society that many people moved from dark glasses to the use of masks, from free thought to distraction and entertainment. Since the veil brings bad memories to some, other forms of concealment have proliferated: there are masks for going to the bathroom, masks for sleeping on hot days, or for making love illicitly. There is a mask for everything, and none of them reveals any aspect of the wearer's personality, leading to a perfection in the art of erasing individuality. Because if it is not possible to hide from the Great God-machine, at least it is possible for our fellow humans not to recognize us easily, in the event of the miracle of fame. However, in this process of human abstraction, there is always some insignificant detail that, in the long run, ends up becoming an element of utmost significance. Sometimes it's a mole on a buttock, other times a certain profile of a thigh or shoulders. All of this provoked in people a feeling of sadness and dissatisfaction that was confused with happiness. Yet none of this was inevitable. As often happened in the past, perhaps it would have been enough to simply question the current state of affairs, if not for the fact that Someone had foreseen it, turning it into an enterprise that was at least improbable, since the critics and philosophers had been exterminated, condemned to oblivion, or buried under a tombstone with the same irrefutable inscription: IDIOT. On the contrary, it is possible that the initial solution will continue to be perfected: it won't be long before people are seen on the streets dressed from head to toe, not in thick black cloth as in the East, but perhaps through successive manipulations of personal appearance.]

For a moment, the musician abandons his melancholic thoughts and returns to the small room of the confessional. He looks at the young woman carefully. Judging by her legs, one could say she hasn't even finished high school yet. There are other details that confirm this: her shyness, for example. A minute has passed, and she is still standing, exploring the chamber with her death mask, as if it were the first time she's entered one, peering through the glass as if trying to recognize the white-bearded man seated in a chair against the opposite wall, with a saxophone on his knees and a sad gaze, fixed on nothing. For a moment, she thinks the man is blind, but it's just a fleeting impression. It would be absurd, and besides, he has just moved his eyes toward her feet. That is, he's looking at her. This reminds her that time is passing and she must begin. So she tests the solidity of the glass with her hand, an instinctive movement that only serves to waste more time. She knows it's three centimeters thick and bulletproof, but she tests it with disguised force anyway. She would have preferred a young man for her first time, though there are advantages: it's more disgusting and less frightening. Then she checks that she's locked the door and begins to undress. She is undoubtedly a shy young woman. Her hips haven't yet stood out from the rest of her body: her height dominates, a certain resemblance to a figure from El Greco she saw the previous week at the MOMA, accentuated by the cold light of the confessional, one step away from being confirmed or dismissed by a tragic feeling that threatens to settle on the other side of the glass. He could be her father, her grandfather. But that's how it is. "You desire what you condemn," her friend had told her. "You need to open a release valve, and sex is the valve of morality." But morality was there, to heighten the tension and desire, like that glass that protected her. The mask isn't the most appropriate, the musician thinks. Once, a man committed suicide in a confessional. But it's better not to remember those things now; it's taken him enough time to smooth the sharp edges of some memories. Fine, forgetting is a fashionable art, though poorly practiced: doctors force us to remember the most unpleasant aspects of our existence, what sensitivity has cast into the basements of memory, while media stupidity delights in destroying what remains in the main hall.

Well, she hasn't finished undressing completely, but she stops. She looks through the glass again. The old man who's been assigned to her hasn't moved since she entered.

He's not blind. He's not dead either. They could have tricked her with a mannequin, one of those animated holograms that were once in fashion, before real men returned. But no; he's as alive as he is sad. His sadness spreads through the glass. It's like poverty: it splashes. A friend had told her that men, as soon as they see women enter, press themselves against the glass, almost always exposing themselves, and sooner or later end up soiling it. Once, she'd even encountered a woman who bit the glass as if she were rabid, right where other men had done their business, spreading their idiotic semen. From this story, the almost impossible image of a woman biting glass on the flat side had stayed in her mind, until at another friend's house she saw a dog doing the same to ask its owner to open the back door.

That's what she'd been told about men. This old man wasn't like that. So she felt completely safe and finished undressing. She stood close to the glass and turned halfway, the tips of her feet resisting the turn. Then she looked at him for a moment. There was nothing to fear, because just as the security of those chambers was rigorous, so was the hygiene: a minute after the room was vacated, it was automatically filled with disinfectant radiation, so there was no chance of any contagion. In fact, no cases of contagion were known, which is why the Ministry of Health certified the safety of the Confessionals every year. On the other hand, or perhaps for the same reason, the Central Government invested almost half its annual budget in a moralizing campaign that has since become part of the collective consciousness, promoting the practice of masturbation. Undoubtedly, all scientific studies had demonstrated the hygienic advantages of this habit, to which the benefits of cloning and assisted reproduction, later called "controlled reproduction," were added. Once the shame of being filmed in a masturbatory act was removed, thanks to the government's and private institutions' re-moralizing campaign on Sexual Relations, pornography gained a predominant place in society and in the psychology of the average citizen. Everything that represented an advancement in the natural need for freedom that exists in every human being. It did not diminish interest in sex; on the contrary, it only led to a true revolution in sexual practice, with the curious elimination of intercourse among the educated class.

He was also watching her, though now his eyes showed surprise, more surprise than disinterest. She insisted and went much further: with her heart racing, she removed her mask and looked him in the eyes. A lively smile appeared on his face, a second before the buzzer sounded. Exceeding the time limit by even a minute would mean paying for a new ticket, so the young woman hurriedly grabbed the clothes on the floor, dressed, and left without looking back.

The musician left without the same haste, noticing that the young woman had forgotten her mask on the floor. He imagined that at that very moment she would be exiting onto Fifth Avenue, while his path slowly led him to Sixth. On Fifth, she might take a taxi and disappear among the ten million anonymous inhabitants of the city. He would never see that smile again, the one he had been waiting to see (he thought this now) for years, since the confessionals were invented. For years he had seen women of all kinds, sometimes men, rehearsing and repeating those poses that were supposed to be considered obscene, waiting furiously for him to react by trying to break the unbreakable glass, or something like that, as if they needed some of the danger they avoided in the confessionals.

To be more precise, he had been waiting for that smile since he arrived in New York, over forty years ago. It was the smile, even the gaze, the gesture, the ghostly presence of that young woman he had loved over forty years ago. That is to say, perhaps no one had entered the twin chamber of the confessional the last time, but rather his tormented imagination, feverish from the first cold of the winter of 2055, which almost killed him, preventing him from working in Central Park and, worse, plunging him into a deep and understandable nostalgia of an old man.

Tacuarembó, 2000

The pure fire of ideas

The rat passes defiantly in front of the fire, with the step of a hunter. The movements of a feline, of a philosopher. Not of a rat. I'm surprised it's not afraid of me. It woke me with the noise it made gnawing on one of the books I forgot on the floor before falling asleep. Or perhaps it fell from my hands and landed a few inches from the fire that burns as if time were repeating itself in its hell. Nine-thirty.

I mistook the sound of its teeth on the book's cover for the destruction of the firewood. As a child, I confused the night wind through the tree branches with the waves of the sea among the rocks. Then I understood that to understand was to devalue the metaphor. To unveil the metaphor with words that, in turn, were each an ancient hidden metaphor, with a long history of waves and winds trying to explain the invisible. Or worse: what is seen.

Luckily, it woke me. The rat. Tonight I had a terrible dream. I'm not superstitious; I only suspect the subconscious. My ideas are changing. My language. For the worse, I now realize. I've stopped believing in the value of inconsistency. How long, Mr. Unamuno? Your odes to contradiction, your praises of rhetorical doubt and your abuse of metaphors: if money is good for the body, ideas are good for the spirit, since ideas are like money. But who said ideas are like money? He did, of course, Mr. Unamuno. But try telling him something; he'll have to listen to you for an hour before kindly kicking you out. He'll prefer the latter, I assure you.

Before or after sitting by the fire, I had been reading, with annoyance, an attack on *Ideocracy*, published in 1944. Without a doubt, this is the central part of my nightmare. A letter addressed to my friend Ramiro de Maeztu. Before or after, I fell asleep by the fire and dreamed that my foot was on fire. Literally, my foot was aflame, and I couldn't move it. Ulysses was there, my cat, between the fire and me, probably outside the dream. Ulysses disappeared in the blink of an eye; perhaps he was chasing a woman's cry coming from the street. I also wanted to go see and couldn't. An infinite weariness prevented me. I thought someone would come to my aid, but I could only watch as the flames climbed up the fabric of my pants. At first, I felt a bit of pain, and then almost nothing. A door slamming violently in the wind and little else. I was comforted by the thought that it could no longer slam, that the draft would no longer threaten me with one of those horrible plagues that make people uncomfortable, and that I wouldn't have to get up anymore.

Now let's return to what matters. I don't remember ever writing that letter, that incendiary little essay, according to the footnote, 36 years ago. Then—or was it before?—I dreamed that I was reading an essay I had written myself, in which I publicly defended the value of money as collective consciousness and the value of pure ideas as guides of the spirit, which are not life and form but essence. It was a dream, a warning from a subconscious that is becoming wiser than my own consciousness, than my true self. It was a dream and something more. It must have been a dream because Ulysses wasn't there, and the woman was crying without stopping. But it would have been just another dream, absurd like almost all of them, if I hadn't woken up agitated, on the verge of an attack, sweating, and embraced by the flames of hell. The woman, the rat, the fire, *Ideocracy*. It would have been just another dream if it had only been the dream of this early morning and not the same dream I had seven days ago, which still disturbs my reason. It would have been just another dream if, instead of defending the idea of money as *collective consciousness*, I had attacked it, and if instead of my signature and a future date at the bottom—December 1944—it had said 1907 or 1920.

Now I know. It's a warning. How did I not realize it before? My ideas are changing *dangerously*. My adversaries, who have always fought for the Republic or for the Monarchy, have always taken all the risks, even the cowardly and miserable risk of death. But they never went through this, I'm sure. They were never afraid to one day change one of those ideas that served to put their own lives at risk. The fortune of fools, but fortune nonetheless! Fools share symbols like "the homeland," "freedom," "ideals," and "honor," but they kill each other over their meanings. And I, the devil knows, have lived for a long time proud of my philosophical principle of impunity in contradiction. The heroic coherence of being contradictory all my life, because men are contradictory, because life is. Because the reasons of the *heart* are not those of the *air*, but the reasons of the *ass*... But perhaps now I realize, everything can be contradictory, except a philosopher.

I should take note of this before I forget. Later, I spend the whole day trying to remember an idea I conceived in a dream or just before falling asleep, and which for some reason I considered key to unraveling a mystery that is never resolved. But when I'm falling asleep, I don't have the strength to recover and take up pen and paper. I know my weaknesses as a problematic worm, and that's why I always have a pen by the bed, on the nightstand or on the floor, in the pocket of my pants or in my shirt. It's also true that when I need it most, I can't find it or can't reach it. When I don't have paper, I write on my left hand, on my arm, or on my navel. When I don't have a pen, I mess up the nightstand to remind myself when I wake up that I must remember something. I often succeed. It's as if I'm speaking directly with an old acquaintance, the one I will be tomorrow or someday. Like at this very moment. I should take note of all this, but how should I write it to protect myself from the dialectical terrorist who, in nine years, will raise his sword against these, which will be his old ideas? I'll resort to fiction. A story, for example, that faithfully describes this precise moment. Something so incomprehensible that it becomes irrefutable. I'll remember this moment, though my usual critics will say it's a dirty fiction overloaded with ideas. I won't care; they've always said the same, and I've always kept doing the same. That my style is clumsy, that I have no style or that I repeat the same devices, that I contradict myself or that I can't define what I think. But if all that is true, it's no less true that few like me have left blood on the page. I am more important than my writings, than my ideas, and my critics do nothing but confirm it, insult after insult. But in the end, they are always them, in the plural for History, and Unamuno is me. That is, the only adversary I can fear is myself, the one I will be in nine years.

Nine thirty-three. I've already woken up, I'm sitting but I can't move to take the pen. It's as if I don't want to either. The anguish, the anxiety of the nightmare in the form of text, lingers. But I'm not crying; the woman cries for me. My face must be the same stone as always, expressionless, carved like a madness of Gaudí. I just stare at my right foot, which has started to burn. It's a very small flame, but that's how all great fires begin. Like... And yet, I'm not worried. I'd even say that in its fierce beauty lies a small hope. Why should I worry if it doesn't even hurt? At another time, I would have kicked hard or torn off my shoe. As if it were something truly urgent. It's not, of course. The urgent must always be the most important, and the most important thing is to figure out how to avoid becoming the person I will be in 1944, how to avoid getting lost in the ambiguous hell of history, where Genghis Khan, the false Alfonso III, and the true Ortega y Gasset ride.

Ulysses isn't here. He's simply gone, as illogical as it seems. That's his place, I've seen him defend it tooth and nail. He hates the cold of this season, but he hates even more when someone usurps his territory. His rug. I mistook his absence for a dream, but I must think that he's simply gone in search of the woman. Cats are creatures of the night, of dreams. That is, I can't be dreaming of his absence. But his rug is unprotected, and a rat has run over it.

I don't want to see this as another premonition, as a symbol or a metaphor that only mystics see in very acute states of the spirit. It just makes me think of many things. I think, for example, of my own absence. This shouldn't concern someone who has long since earned Paradise or Hell. I'm not thinking of my death, but of my *absence*. In 1944, I'll still be writing, but I'll be absent. And my enemies will step on my rug with impunity. I could never publish this last part; the rats would accuse me of arrogance, and nothing is harder to refute than the whining of a horde of rats when they're swept away by the current.

I must avoid dissolving into chaos, and for that, I find myself in the difficult position of no longer refuting or contradicting what I've affirmed elsewhere and at another time, when I was supposedly more ignorant than today and less wise, but rather I must refute something I'll say with fury and conviction ten years from now.

It's a completely new task. I've spent the best part of my life refuting who I was years ago, with the authority of maturity. Never, I must believe, have I felt the obligation to fight who I will be in an unknown and unimaginable time. I'll have to do it now, also from the superiority of maturity, but with the terrible disadvantage of others' incomprehension: few or no one will accept that who I will be will be inferior to who I am, that who I will be in eight years will be a philosopher in decline, a man suddenly senile, with the always deceptive pretense of greater experience, with the religious abuse conferred by a whiter beard and a more lost gaze, an incomprehensible voice. Because our Europe still trusts more in old age than in youth. As for Spain, don't even mention it; it's not trust we have for the old but fear, deep fear of the young. I myself wanted to be old at twenty. I imitated the weariness of the old while patiently waiting for the first white streaks in my beard. But deep down, my spirit was always young. Light, euphoric, contradictory. Of course, it's easy to say that now that I'm irremediably an old man. I can no longer expect encouraging changes in my body. Much less in my mind, in this tired mind that threatens to lose control. Tired and, what's worse, disillusioned.

Nine thirty-three. It hasn't been long, then, since the woman started crying; it hasn't been long since Ulysses left and the rat came after to rescue me from that nightmare.

If only I believed it was just a dream and nothing more... But I should realize that not only am I on the path to destroying all my current convictions, but I also risk switching to the enemy's side, to the side of those politicians and thinkers who, on this side and the other of the Atlantic, defend the idea of the divine nature of money, of the sciences and pure ideas, of armed struggle and class struggle. The fire could destroy who I am not yet, who I will be after today, but the person I will be tomorrow could destroy everything I've been until now, and I won't be present to defend myself. It's always been this way without anyone noticing. For this reason, no one can claim that with time men become more lucid, but it is certain that they grow more cowardly... Perhaps that is why this dream, this mysterious revelation, distresses me so much.

Everyone knows I hate pure ideas, the ideas that govern us. I've said it before. I say it once more only so as not to forget it, before I sink into the apparent, into the unconsciousness of who I will become. But it's no use writing it down. I have written too much, in vain. Later, it has served me to pour fresh ink fire over the faded ink on the paper. What will my friends, my disciples, my followers say when they see me (once again) change without shame? If I had lost faith in God, I could still preach, convinced that belief, true or deceptive, is good for people. But when one stops believing in the ideas they believed in until yesterday, ideas that until yesterday were useful and beneficial, they lose all reason to continue defending them.

It's true that one changes with the years, changes ideas as one changes clothes. One changes, Unamuno changes. What a novelty. As for physical changes, I'd rather not speak. That's what doctors and whining old women are for. But something remains the same, and it must be the spirit. Whether by truth or illusion, one expects from it the opposite of the shameful spectacle of the body, and perhaps that is why one becomes a philosopher. To conquer death, to distract or to despise pain. The men who pass through the entrance of the cave are real, but the shadows are no less so. *No more, no less.* (Do not forget to underline that *no more, no less*; it's so fashionable now to attribute more reality to the shadows than to the bodies that cast them.) But we men, with our old warrior obsessions, turn every new idea into a new weapon of combat, and our identity into a trench. Then it's no longer enough to affirm something new; it's also necessary to deny something old. Or everything else.

If only the rat I will become had this lucidity and left standing this last thing I'm saying, which I hadn't said until today. But no. I assure you it won't. I will deny myself again, destroy myself, sink into shame and the ridicule of others. The rat will gnaw away at the best of what I was, the best I left to humanity. *I won't be present to defend myself from myself.*

That's why it's time to act. I already have a precise strategy. From today onward, and for as long as my lucidity allows, I will articulate a thought that justifies all the madness to come. In fact, everything I say in the future, while trying to deny my current ideas, must be *confirmations*, not of the ideas I will have but of the ideas I defend today, confirmations of the ideas I will pretend to deny. I could begin by saying, "to prove this hypothesis, I myself will attack it in ten years, I myself will affirm the opposite."

I will stop attacking the poor thinker I was ten years ago and begin attacking the perverse thinker I will become in the years to come. Of course, some fool will think, how can I know if the lucid thinker is the one I am today? Simply, my dear reader, because one must act according to their convictions. And if I was able to foresee this problem today and not yesterday or tomorrow, it must be because today I am the best of the three I was and will be. Today I am the best of the three Unamunos, and therefore, the one I am today will win. If tomorrow I am not able to dismantle the plan I conceive today, I won't be worth the effort. I, the true I, the best of the I's, the most lucid, will prevail. Truth lies in success, triumph is truth. For this logical reason, I am not willing to listen to anyone but myself. Not even the others I am not right now, here and now.

I will begin this very night. Or perhaps tomorrow, when I am more recovered. I am very tired, like a sculptor who has had to struggle for a long time with a great block of stone to rescue from its depths a delicate image of a woman, of the virgin with her fallen son in her arms. I have been trying to wake up for three minutes. Or more, because it's likely the clock has stopped. It's stuck at nine thirty-three. I don't want to speculate on this fact, but I'm starting to do things inevitably. At thirty-three, I had my spiritual crisis. At the same age, Jesus and all the other spiritual leaders who have survived death.

Well, enough, let's get to work. As soon as I can move, I will move. As soon as I can escape this hell, I will escape. Unless the fire makes the completion of such a brilliant task unnecessary, unless...

I saw the rat retrace its steps and pass between my feet. It had bloodstains on its snout, though I couldn't say for certain. My deep exhaustion, the hellish light of the fire distorts the colors, and the rat has disappeared beneath my armchair where the small flame at my right foot burns. All I hear is the sound of its teeth gnawing at the book's covers, its pages, as if it were flesh or paper burning in a wood stove. It's likely that the fire isn't even necessary.

Athens, 2005

The Choice

Dad, we need to talk. I know what I'm about to say will be hard for you, but I also know that with time you'll learn to accept it…

Your wife and I are going to separate. Both of us are going to form new families. You'll come with me and live with Amalia. Amalia is the mom I met at daycare. Remember that woman with black hair who always came with a blond boy who wore glasses? Well, that's her. It wasn't love at first sight. It was something that developed over time. I don't know how to explain it to you. I know that right now you're probably thinking, "How is it possible for a daughter to stop loving one mother and start loving another?" But there are things, feelings that children have that an adult could never understand. Surely when you're old, you'll manage to understand it. The elderly remember their childhood better than the rest of their lives, marked by confusion and the fantasies of adults. That's why I'm asking you not to try to understand everything. Just accept it as it is, since it's a decision that's already been made. The longer you take, the more you'll suffer.

Amalia has a five-year-old son, almost the same age as me, so I'm sure you'll learn to love him just as Mom will learn to love Ignacio's girl as if she were me.

We've already talked about it with your wife. Sometimes the relationship between a child and one of their parents doesn't work out, and the best thing, to avoid conflicts that harm both, is separation.

You know that things between Mom and I haven't been good for a long time. Once, she even spanked me because I spilled coffee on her computer. That damn computer that destroyed our mother-daughter relationship. I didn't report it to the schoolteacher to avoid taking things to an extreme that could harm her even more. The spanking, that primitive reaction, typical of caveman parents, was just the last straw. We decided to separate on good terms. Yes, I know you love your wife, but you'll learn to live without her and to love Amalia as you love Mom. You'll be able to visit her on weekends. What do you expect? There's no middle ground. I can't live with your wife anymore, and you can't live with her and me under the same roof. Imagine her having to cross paths every morning with my new mother, and me having to see her new children hugging her and covering her with kisses, and her happily fulfilled as a mother. Deep down, I couldn't stand it either, no matter how fair it is.

No, it's also not possible to have a third house where you and Mom can live alone. I need a father, and you need me too. When I turn eighteen, then yes, you'll be free and can go back to Mom if you want. I'm still a child, and I have the right to rebuild my life. You're an adult, you've already lived a big part of your life, you have experience, and this change won't traumatize you. You'll learn to accept it with time.

You'll also have to be an understanding and sensible father. Amalia has her flaws and virtues, but she's a good woman and a good mother. She's not good at cooking, so I hope you'll learn to cook for the four of us, and when she does cook, you'll have the decency to praise her effort.

I know this takes you a bit by surprise, though you've probably guessed it for some time now. I know it's not easy to have to live with and love another mother as you loved your wife. It's not about replacing your feelings. You'll still love your wife as always, but you'll also have to learn to live with another wife and do your best to love her as I love her.

Imagine how absurd it would be if it were you, the father, who decided to leave with another woman, and I, the child, who had to face and adapt to a similar problem, an adult's problem, an adult's whim? I'd have to love a new mom that you chose. Maybe I couldn't handle it, because I'm a very young child. But you're an adult, and you'll know how to adapt. Of course, that's how it was in the savage societies of your great-great-grandparents, but fortunately, today we children have our rights secured. We are no longer little woolen sacks where adults unload all their whims and frustrations. It will be my turn when I'm an adult to protect my children from my loves and heart-breaks.

I know it hurts, that your old heart will struggle to accept it, but there's no turning back. You'll have to learn to love Amalia just as I'll learn to love Pablito as if he were my brother. In fact, he's going to be my brother from today on. You'll see that Amalia is a charming wife...

What can you do, Dad? Don't cry. That's just how life is.

Athens, 2007